About the Author

B. J. Edwin was born in 1984 in Sweden where he has been living. His main body of work consists of short stories and poems, and he has a soft spot for classic horror movies.

Play With Me

B.J. Edwin

Play With Me

Vanguard Press

VANGUARD

© Copyright 2024
B.J. Edwin

The right of B.J. Edwin to be identified as author of
this work has been asserted by him in accordance with the
Copyright, Designs and Patents Act 1988.

All Rights Reserved

No reproduction, copy or transmission of this publication
may be made without written permission.
No paragraph of this publication may be reproduced,
copied or transmitted save with the written permission of the publisher,
or in accordance with the provisions
of the Copyright Act 1956 (as amended).

Any person who commits any unauthorized act in relation to this
publication may be liable to criminal prosecution and civil claims for
damages.

A CIP catalogue record for this title is available from the British Library.

ISBN 970-1-83704-241-1

This is a work of fiction. Names, characters, businesses, places, events
and incidents are either the products of the author's imagination or used
in a fictitious manner. Any resemblance to actual persons, living or
dead, or actual events is purely coincidental.

Vanguard Press is an imprint of
Pegasus Elliot Mackenzie Publishers Ltd.
www.pegasuspublishers.com

First Published in 2024

Vanguard Press
Sheraton House Castle Park
Cambridge England

Printed & Bound in Great Britain

Dedication

For my sons and loving wife.

Contents

The Mark of a Noose 11

On the Brink of Madness 21

Shed Skin 36

Bodies 50

Darkness 62

My Own Mental Mansion 76

Drowned and Buried 89

Happy Birthday 102

My Lady in the Painting 114

Play with Me 127

Pest 137

Here Lies Walter Smith 154

In bloom 163

The Manifest 169

The Birth of a Psychopath 179

The Mark of a Noose

How strange that I would find myself in front of the very house where my father was found hanging from the ceiling and my mother stuck her head in the gas oven leaving me to become an orphan. My grandfather also ended his days in this house with his lips tightly wrapped around a gun.

I could go on and on about family members and distant relatives who have died in this very house. Not so strange considering that my family has owned the estate for many hundred of years, but the remarkable thing is not that they died, but how they did so for a vast majority of these people committed suicide. And yet, I feel obliged to add, we have no record of mental illness in the family. All suicides have come extremely rapidly and without any warning or explanation.

Therefore, I very early decided that I did not want anything to do with the house at all, which is why it was left for my sister, while I indulged myself in the big city life for many years. I would be lying if I did not tell you that it was with a great deal of agony that I received a letter from my sister's lawyer telling me that she had fallen off the roof. He called it an accident, but I know better. There are no accidents in this house and there never has been though they might have appeared as such.

Apart from my sister, I am the last heir of the estate and, therefore, she left everything to me. I know that she would have chosen otherwise had she been able to do so, but this house does things to you and your mind. Horrible things that you would not wish to your greatest enemy, and I am certain that not long after her unfortunate move to the house, the decay of her soul began.

I saw glimpses of her downfall throughout the years although I never visited her. Her phone calls became rarer and when she finally would make contact with me, it was short and odd conversations that made no sense. At one point she called me in the middle of the night breathing heavily, hissing "they are coming for me" and then she slammed the phone in my ear.

In sheer panic, I called the cops who drove up to her house and searched the entire place, but no one was to be found except for my honestly surprised sister who had no recollection of our phone call whatsoever. This was one of many similar events where I feared for her life.

I have never in my life tried to force my sister to do anything. She has always been a strong person with a solid mind and a healthy way of life, but at one point I tried to make her leave the house. I hired a truck to come and pick her stuff up and told her to get dressed and wait for a cab that could get her from that wretched place. She refused and accused me of interfering with her personal life against her will. She added a couple of colorful nicknames for me and then she hung up the phone.

I knew very well what I was doing, and I even have to agree that I actually was trying to control her, but, in my defense, that house is not sane. Not the least and as I have said before, I really feared for my sister's health and life. She remained in the house completely unaware of the horrid fact that it was consuming her from within, drawing her to the brink of insanity.

Finally, she must have snapped and jumped off the roof in desperation as if there were no other way out. I know that something made her do it since the only way up on the roof is a hatch in the ceiling which she could not possibly have reached all by herself. Something forced her up there and made her jump, of that I am sure.

Believe me when I say that the feelings that went through my body when I was told by my sister's lawyer that my sister had left me the estate in her will were indescribable. It was as if someone had smashed something extremely heavy against my head and I felt nauseous. One part of me wanted to run away while another part of me wanted to scream my insides out. Just the very thought of having to be listed as an owner of that ill-forsaken house had me shaken deeply.

My first idea was to have everything just leveled to the ground in my absence. That felt like a safe way to be rid of the horrid legacy of my family once and for all. It sounded so good that I looked up the telephone number to a demolition company right away. Then, in the middle of the phone call, I stopped myself. After all, there were a lot of things in that house that I wanted to save. Things from our childhood reminded me of the good times I had had with my sister, and I felt like I needed them. I decided that

I would go there and collect her belongings first and then have a bulldozer tear the mansion down to the very core.

The more I thought about it, the better it sounded. It was a dream I had had for many years without even knowing it and now I felt that it had to be done. I would stand by the side of the house and laugh while crying tears of joy and when the house was gone, I would grab some gasoline and a match and send the whole thing down to the hell flames from whence it came.

I made all the necessary arrangements with the demolition company and then I went up to the house to get the belongings. The road was long and not even my GPS could show me the entire way. Finally, I came to a small village which seemed to be the last place that was on the map. I stopped an elderly lady on the sidewalk to ask for directions.

I explained to her who I was, and as soon as she heard my name, I swear I could see a little twitch in her left eye, and she seemed to be pondering my question as if she was not sure what I had said.

"I said, my name is Gregory Williams. Do you know the way to my family's estate?" I repeated.

"I heard you the first time," the old lady snapped at me. "Drive up along that graveled path you see up ahead. It's narrow and you have to follow it for quite a while, but you can't miss it." I thanked her, and just as I was about to leave, I thought I heard her muttering, "May God have mercy on your soul." An uneasy feeling grew within me as I went further up the very narrow path. The lady had not been lying. The road was truly long and almost impossible to drive on and I had to do my best to avoid the razor-sharp stones that pointed up like spikes along the road.

After a good while, I could see the manor coming up on me as a horrid deformity in the middle of the forest. Before I walked inside, I decided to have a look around. There was the hatch on the rooftop which my sister had climbed out of, and I could even see where she had slipped a bit because there were several broken tiles that had fallen to the ground. Then I saw the place where she had "jumped". The police had done a pretty decent job taking care of the mess but there were still traces and I could see clearly where her body had been.

After having cried a few tears, I decided to get on with my mission. The hour grew late and the demolition company said that they would be here the very next morning, so I needed to be quick about it. I went inside only to find myself warped through time and space for I soon realized that my sister had turned the house into a complete replica of our childhood home. In all its absurdity it was a museum, no, a mausoleum over my family's tragic fate and history. I shuddered and felt both nauseated and disgusted.

With a speed so fast that you would think I was chased by a demon, I wrapped up the most important belongings and left the rest to be destroyed. As I came out to my car, I saw to my dismay that all of my tires were flat. I sighed and looked at my watch. It was late. Very late and no repair shop would be open until tomorrow. As much as I abhorred it, I could see no other choice than to spend the night in the manor and call someone in the morning and so, with great reluctance, I decided to stay.

As I wandered around the corridors of the manor, I felt a growing sense of disgust and fear for the walls were literally covered with old, framed photos of family members deceased since long together with recent family pictures. To some, nothing more than personal photos and memories but to me, it was like looking at photos from a mental institution. It was there, in every picture if you looked closely. A strange madness in all their eyes. A madness that sooner or later must have driven them all to suicide. There was something deeply disturbing and most horrifying. The way they stared at you through the photos as if they could see you. Even feel you.

For some reason, I could not help myself from going through the entire house as if I had a need to actually see everything no matter what. I came out into the big hall and gazed straight up toward the beam that had been the choice of death for so many of my relatives. You could even see the mark where they all had tied up the noose. The wood was abraded and had a significantly lighter tone. A shiver went through my body as I thought about the many lives that had ended with a noose wrapped tight around their necks.

With no intention of stopping longer than needed, I hurried on until I came to the library. The only place not smeared with macabre remnants of repressed memories. Here I decided that it was safe, and I saw no reason to leave the library until morning.

I decided to crash on the couch since I wanted nothing to do with any of the bedrooms upstairs. It was bad enough that I had to stay in the house which had become the crypt and the curse of my family but I sure as hell did not intend to sleep in my dead sister's bed.

It was pitch dark and I felt exhausted but still, I could not find enough peace to get any kind of rest. Not a single sound was to be heard. Not even the nocturnal sounds of owls or rats which you would normally hear in an old house. Instead, there was an unnatural silence surrounding the entire place as if nothing dared to go near the premises. I tried to listen really hard just to feel a bit safer but after having listened too focused I got a headache and decided to stop. The night felt as long as several days and I found myself staring into the ceiling just waiting for dawn to come.

After a good while, I fell asleep of complete exhaustion. The tense of being back at the house and all the memories it brought with it had strained my senses to their limits and I fell into sleep. However, it was not a comfortable sleep as I was haunted by dreams from my past. I saw my sister in her white nightgown. She was looking straight at me. Not with a smile and not with hate or anger but with a sense of disappointment as if she felt that she had been abandoned. Abandoned by me since I had left her with the dreaded legacy of our family.

She was crying. I could see that, and, suddenly, she was surrounded by shadows. Some of the figures I could not recognize but Mom and Dad I could see clearly. My sister gazed upon me, and with her lips, she formed a single word: "Help." Then her face got twisted and she stared at me with agony as if her very soul was being tormented. Raped to its dead core. She crouched and then a shriek that could have been heard a mile away had me awoken to gasp for air.

For a good while, I lay on the couch staring into a crack in the ceiling pondering my dream. It had me startled and now I just waited for dawn to come. The wait was tedious but most of all it was horrifying, and the dream had made me terribly paranoid.

All of a sudden, the silence was interrupted by a voice. It was no more than a vague whisper in the dark, but it pierced the dusty air of the halls like a sharp knife. I tried to make out words, but the voice was too remote and slowly I got out of the couch and started walking toward the source. It seemed to come from the hallway and I kept walking in its direction like a moth drawn to its inevitable doom.

The hallway was empty and there was no one to be seen. I tried to listen, but the voice was gone. I decided that everything had been a vision from my dreams, and I turned to go back to the couch. Just when I was about to exit the hallway, I heard something. Not a voice and not a rat within the walls. This was something completely different. A distant click, like a door, silently closing to one of the rooms upstairs.

I cannot say that I was not curious about where the sound came from but I felt like I knew better and instead I decided to go back to the couch. All the way back through the hallway I could not help but sense that I was being watched. A feeling I had not had just a while ago. My presence had stirred something up in the house. Of that I was sure and for some reason, I knew that it was linked to the dreadful fate of my family.

I wish that I could say that sleep eluded me but instead I fell asleep immediately as if I was being drawn toward deep and involuntary sleep. In my sleep, I dreamed dreams too ghastly and obscene to even begin to describe. The only thing I can say is that they felt far too real to be only dreams and no matter how unreal it may sound I could swear that the visions were eating their way through my very brain, twisting my perception of reality.

Suddenly, I was awakened only to find myself tucked in my sister's bed. I sat up straight and gasped for air. Breathing did not come easy to me, and for every breath I took, it felt like my lungs were filled with thick, black mold.

With a horrible feeling running down my spine to the very core of my bones I literally jumped out of bed. My eyesight became blurry and, for a second, it felt like I was about to faint. I tried getting a grip and then I made my way to the bedroom door. It was locked from the outside. With as much strength as I could muster, I slammed my entire weight against the door, but it would not budge an inch. Exhausted from all the tension I fell to the floor and buried my face in the palm of my hands. This was surely it. The house had gotten me and now I faced the same fate as the rest of my family. The bedroom that had been my sisters would now be my tomb. Tomorrow they would come to tear the house to pieces only to find my dead corpse mutilated beyond recognition.

How stupid I had been to think that I would survive even a single night there. Slowly I let my future carcass fall to the floor and there I lay dying in my own self-pity when all of a sudden there was another click, and the door was pushed open. I say pushed for it was clear that it was no coincidence that I could now escape.

As I came out in the hall, I saw the tie beam once again and tied around it was a rope with a noose at the end. The mere sight had me startled and I fell down the staircase whereon everything went black.

When I finally came to, I was shocked to find that I was balancing on the rail to the indoor balcony with my head inside the very noose I had just seen and all around me, I swear I could see glimpses of my relatives pushing me to jump.

On the Brink of Madness

Meredith Brown looked in the mirror again. She examined every detail carefully. She was wearing a black suit and her hair was tied to a knot. It was the first day of her internship and she wanted to make a professional impression.

She was to spend her internship at Spring Forest Asylum. A small institution which she had never heard of before. The whole place was run by a psychiatrist named Albert Hart. She had booked a meeting with him and was on her way there now.

The internship was six weeks long and a part of her education. She wanted to become a psychiatrist just like Albert Hart. It was a five-year-long education and she had finished the first two years. Now she was excited to see a real institution and meet some real patients. Meredith grabbed her coat and went out to her car.

The road was long and seemed to take her away from the cities and the communities and out into the forest. There was less traffic here and there had been no houses for many miles. After just an hour or so, it began to rain heavily and after that came a horrible thunderstorm.

In spite of the fact that Meredith had had a driver's license for many years, she still hated to drive in rain. It made it almost impossible to see the road. Suddenly, out of nowhere, was a sign that said "Spring Forest Asylum" and an arrow pointing to a road that was nothing more than a path.

Meredith turned her car up the path and drove on. The road was slippery due to the bad weather. She kept on driving but was afraid to get a flat tire so far away from a city. The rain still poured down making the road extremely muddy.

By some miraculous way, Meredith was able to get the car all the way up to the asylum without as much as a scratch on the car. She parked it outside the gates and walked up to ring the bell.

The asylum was like something out of a nightmare. It was on top of a hill with nothing but forest surrounding it. Large iron gates guarded the asylum and great bolts of lightning struck down upon the terrifying building. Meredith felt a chill go through her spine and for a moment she did not want to go inside.

After all, it rained a lot and she wanted to get herself dry as fast as possible. She rang the bell and a woman dressed in a white lab coat came running out with an umbrella.

"You must be Meredith Brown," the woman said.

"Yes, that's right. I am," Meredith responded.

"I'm Joanne Walker and I am the superintendent of Spring Forest Asylum. Follow me. We must hurry inside. You'll catch a cold out here." They went inside and Joanne shoved Meredith to a bathroom. "There are clean towels there and a hair dryer right there," Joanne said, pointing with her finger. "Let me know when you are done, and I will take you to see the doctor."

Meredith was glad to be inside and somewhat dry again. She thanked Joanne who took her to see Doctor Hart right away. He had a big office that looked more like an old library rather than an office and he was sitting in a leather chair taking notes in what seemed to be a patient's file. When he saw Joanne come in with Meredith, he quickly closed the file.

"Ah, Joanne, good that you are here. I've just written that Mr. Williams should be given a larger dose of tranquilizers. He is both a danger to himself and to others in this state."

"Yes, Doctor. Very good," Joanne quickly replied.

"And feel free to put him in the isolation chamber in case he starts screaming again. He is alarming the other patients."

"Yes, however, I doubt that will be necessary."

"Yes, but you'll never know," Doctor Hart replied. Then he turned to Meredith who had been standing by the side quietly. "Ah, and you must be Meredith Brown. Welcome to Spring Forest, Miss Brown!" Hart smiled and shook Meredith's hand and Joanne left the room. "Thank you, Joanne!" Hart said as she left.

"It was not easy getting here," Meredith said, trying to start a conversation.

"No, I understand what you mean completely. This place is very far out into the forest but that's the way we want it. It gives the patients peace and quiet. You see, our category of patients would not do well close to a city with all the noises and the movement. Our patients are best off with solitude, a place away from everything." As Hart finished the last sentence, he gave Meredith a broad smile. There was something about his smile that she did not like but she ignored that feeling.

"And what exactly is your category of patients, Doctor? I tried to find some information about this institution but found very little."

"Oh, we choose not to market ourselves too much, I'm afraid. As for our category of patients. Well, here we deal with what society would call the worst kind, murderers. Homicidal psychopaths to be more precise. People who have committed the worst crimes you could possibly imagine are here, Miss Brown." Hart went silent for a while to let that information sink in. "How are you feeling?" he asked.

"I'm fine. I fully understand and it is not going to be a problem. In fact, I feel excited to be here and to have a chance to learn more about these patients."

"That's the spirit! That's the kind of attitude we want from people who work here. Miss Brown, I think you'll fit in just fine here. I'll have someone show you to your room and then you'll get something to eat before your very first round." Hart smiled once again, and every time he did, Meredith could not help but feel a chill go through her entire body.

Meredith stood in the hallway of her new room. It was small like the rooms in a dorm and had nothing more than a bed, a desk with a wooden chair, and a tiny closet. It wasn't much but it was enough for the few weeks that she was going to stay.

"You'll get used to it," a voice behind her said. It was Joanne who had brought supper. "There is also a common room for the staff a little further down the hall where you can watch T.V. if you like. There is even a library downstairs but that is for both patients and personnel."

"Thank you," Meredith said, "that sounds great."

"I have your supper. You can eat it here or in the dining room. It's down the hall to your right. In half an hour the evening round starts, and I was told by Doctor Hart that you would join us and observe."

"Yes, that's right," Meredith answered between the bites of burrito that was on her plate. Meredith had had many burritos in her days, but this one definitely won first prize for the most tasteless burrito. It did not taste bad; it simply did not taste just about anything. Not even the tomatoes tasted much as strange as it may sound.

Meredith swallowed the last piece of food and looked over at Joanne who had been standing in the doorway waiting for her to finish eating. When she saw that Meredith had finished, she exited the room and got ready to show her the way down.

"Can I give you a little piece of advice?" Joanne asked.

Meredith nodded.

"Try not to get emotional around the patients. All of them are here for crimes that you and I would consider so inhuman that it is easy to let your personal emotions take over but remember that these are sick people," said Joanne.

"I will act professional, don't worry about that," Meredith answered. Joanne looked over at Meredith and smiled. Meredith was not sure, but she felt like it was the same strange smile that Hart had given her.

As they came down the stairs, Doctor Hart was waiting for them along with a few nurses and a couple of security guards. Meredith was glad to see a few other faces as she had found this place to be far more deserted than she had imagined. Just the feeling of being around other people felt nice.

"Excellent! Now that everyone is here, we can begin the evening round and for you who do not know, Meredith came just a few hours ago and is going to do her internship here with us." There were a few who said hello to her. "Meredith, do not hesitate to ask questions and feel free to take notes, you're here to learn. Let's go," Hart said, not expecting a response and then he let the group down the hall to the first cell.

"I hate myself and what I've done," the words came from the very back of a dark room. No person was to be seen but whoever sat there repeated the words over and over again like a broken record. Meredith read the little plaque just next to the door. "Angela White," it said.

"What is her story?" Meredith asked.

"Awful story, actually. She tormented her boyfriend for hours, flogging him and beating him in the most brutal way possible," Hart answered.

"That's terrible," Meredith said, mostly because it seemed like the right thing to say.

"Yes, but that's not all," Hart continued. "When he simply could not take it any more, she mutilated his body and cut him up to tiny pieces." Meredith looked at Hart and gazed into the cell and the person sitting in the corner repeating the words to herself. This was not what she expected from her first internship.

Next was a patient named Adam Wilson. He was in a restraining jacket throwing himself from one wall to another. When he saw that the hatch on the door to the cell opened, he stared right into the light to see who was there. Hart moved away to let Meredith have a look at him.

"This patient can be a bit wild so be extra careful around him," Hart told Meredith.

"Is he the one you prescribed more tranquilizers to earlier?"

"No, that was for Mr. Williams. We'll get to him later."

"So, what is the background of Mr. Wilson?" Meredith asked.

"Mr. Wilson here hung his entire family from a tree in the backyard. Not even the dog was spared." Hart lowered his head as if the subject alone pained him. "Horrible. Just horrible," he muttered to himself. "Anyway, let's move on, shall we?"

The group moved on inspecting every patient one by one discussing everything from behavior to medication. Meredith found it all interesting and took notes and tried to answer whatever questions Hart might have for her.

It took nearly two hours but finally, they were almost done. Now they were at the final cell. Meredith saw the plaque by the door. "Jack Williams," it said; and under the plaque, there was another saying, "Extremely dangerous. Do not approach."

"This," said Hart, "is the patient I was talking about earlier. Jack Williams. He is by far the most dangerous patient we have in this institution. Never ever can you be alone with him. Do not speak to him, do not confront him, and most of all, do not listen to a word he says."

"Why?"

"He will lie to you and trick you. He is very good at that. Remember that every word he speaks is a lie that he made up to get to you." Hart opened the hatch. As soon as Williams saw that it was Hart, he started screaming in pure rage.

"Liar! Monster! You'll never get away with this! You're a psychopath, you hear me? Maniac!" Hart closed the hatch.

"What a vocabulary he has got, hasn't he?" Hart joked. "You see, Meredith, most of the patients here have come to terms with what they've done, so to speak. There is an acceptance, one might say, to their own nature where most of them have accepted the fact that they are murderers but Williams here—he has not accepted it. He still believes that we are all liars and that he is innocent. That is why he is so dangerous."

"What did he do?" Meredith asked carefully.

"Let's save that for another time, shall we? It's late and I'd hate to give you nightmares," Hart said and somehow Meredith felt that he actually meant it.

They finished the evening round but before Meredith went back to her room she asked if it was possible for her to have a look at some of the patients' files. Hart agreed and said that it would be good for her education and that he would have Joanne bring them to her room. Meredith thanked him and went back to her room.

It must have been long after midnight when Meredith suddenly was awakened by a noise. She could not tell exactly where it came from as they seemed to be far away. Long she lay in her bed trying to listen closely to make out anything, but the noises were too far away. Meredith could not help but feel a bit curious as to where the noise came from. For a moment she tried to make up her mind if she should care but she felt that she needed to know.

Meredith got out of bed and put on a robe and went out in the corridor. The noise seemed to come from downstairs but echoed throughout the building. No One else seemed to bother as she was the only one up. Either they did not care, or they knew about it and ignored it, she thought.

At first, Meredith hesitated but then she decided to follow the sound. There were a few screams, and someone was yelling. She could not hear the whole phrase, but she heard a few words like "liar" and "stop it". There was also another sound. She could not put her finger on what it was, but it sounded like a T.V.

Muffled voices were heard but Meredith could not tell who they belonged to. The entire asylum was dark and only a few lights led the way. Meredith walked very slowly and tried to watch her step. Suddenly, she heard other footsteps than her own and further away there was a flashlight.

Even though she was not a patient here, walking around in the halls at night seemed like a forbidden thing to do and she returned to the room before the guard saw her and became suspicious.

She went back into her room and locked the door behind her. Carefully she listened but it was impossible to hear anything. After almost an hour it became silent again. Completely silent almost like a grave.

Sleep did not come easy to Meredith that night and when the sun finally shone through her window, she felt a relief although she was tired from not sleeping much at all. Exhausted, she forced herself out of bed and out into the dining room for breakfast.

Meredith decided to sit with Tiffany. A nurse who slept in the room right next to hers. Tiffany smiled at Meredith but did not say much. She was not the social kind of person, Meredith thought, but she seemed to be nice.

"Can I ask you something?" Meredith asked. Tiffany nodded. "Did you hear something around midnight? Sounds? Noises? I heard something and it kept me awake the entire night."

"I'm terribly sorry but I'm a heavy sleeper," Tiffany responded quickly. "Not even a train could wake me up," she joked and giggled to herself. Meredith found this very hard to believe but realized that she was not going to get any answers, so she dropped the conversation and ate her breakfast instead.

Meredith had one of the days where she had to study and spent most of her time either in her room by her desk or in the library. She had been at the asylum sometime now and began to know the patients a bit more. She attended all the rounds and had even been at a few treatment sessions.

At the moment, she was sitting in her room reading up on some assignments for school when Joanne suddenly knocked on the door. Under her arm she carried files. Meredith had thought about it a few times, but Joanne always managed to give an insecure impression as if she had to apologize every time she wanted something even though she was the superintendent of the whole institution.

"Here are the patients' files. Doctor Hart said that you wanted them," Joanne said very shortly.

"Perfect! Thank you so much!" Meredith browsed through the files. "There is one missing. Where is Mr. Williams' file?"

"Doctor Hart thought you might ask that," Joanne said with a smile. "That file is restricted and only Doctor Hart has access to it. I'm very sorry."

"That's fine. At least I can read the others." Joanne excused herself one more time and left. Meredith began to read through their journals. Everything was there just like described by the doctor. Angela White, Adam Wilson, and all the others.

Meredith read them all over and over again. Even though everything seemed to be in order. Prescribed medication, exact doses, and all else that should be in a patient's file, Meredith could not shake the feeling that something was horribly wrong. It was hard to say exactly what, but something did not seem right at all. It was almost as if everything was too perfect.

She had attended two of Angela White's treatment sessions and both times she was amazed by how horribly well Angela could remember the night of the murder. Every single detail, every little cut with the knife. It was almost as if she told a story every time. A story she knew so well by heart that she could recite it even in her sleep.

Doctor Hart assured Meredith that this was normal behavior. To go back and replay the scene of the crime to themselves was an important part of their rehabilitation, he argued. He said that the murder becomes almost like a movie inside the person's head playing over and over with no end to it.

Meredith had listened to his words and in some sense, he could be right, but Meredith still felt as if there was another piece of the puzzle missing. A piece deeply hidden within these walls that not a single person dared to speak of. Meredith felt sure of it and was determined to find the missing piece of the puzzle even if it meant having to find a new internship.

After having read the patients' files so many times that she basically knew them by heart, she decided to return them to the doctor. She took the files and went down to his office to return them and perhaps share some of her thoughts with him. As Meredith came down to the office, she saw that the door was open so she went inside.

"Hello? Doctor Hart? Are you here?" There was no response, and no other staff member was close. Meredith put the files on the desk and was just about to leave when her eyes caught something right next to the files. It looked just like more patients' files which seemed impossible since Meredith had had all the originals.

Slowly, she walked up to the files. She made sure that no one was nearby and then she decided to have a quick look. Meredith opened every file one by one, but it made no sense. It was the same patients but, in these pictures, they were wearing regular clothes instead of robes and most of all the names were different. Angela White was named Judy Hill and Andy Wilson was named Frank Lewis. Every single patient that Meredith had seen on rounds was here but their names different.

The text was also changed. Instead of the murders, there were notes on the progress on some kind of treatment that all of them had been subjected to along with strange notes. In Judy Hill's file, it said "Abducted 99-04-08. Came to us with full mental health. No history of medication or other health issues." Meredith looked in the other files. All of them had a date of abduction and were considered to have perfect health.

"Oh, how sad," Meredith heard someone saying behind her. "You were not supposed to see that." It was Doctor Hart who had entered the room without her knowing it.

"What am I looking at? What is going on here?" Meredith asked but feared the answer.

"Oh, come on now! You're a bright young woman. I'm sure you can figure it out."

"These people came to you with perfect health but I've seen them. What have you done to them?"

"Well, you see, it's a little experiment of my own. You see, I've always been fascinated by what exactly makes a murderer, and one day I came up with the brilliant idea to see if I could create murderers out of perfectly healthy people."

"That's not possible!" Meredith said with a trembling voice and tears in her eyes.

"Oh, but I have proof that it is!" Hart said and smiled widely. "You see, we subject our patients to a treatment where we force them to watch a short movie that we've made ourselves of them committing the murder. Then we make them watch that movie hundreds of times, over and over with no sleep. After several hours and days of treatment, they finally start to believe what we want them to believe."

"You're sick! You're a sick monster!" Meredith screamed.

"There, there. Careful now. We wouldn't want you to be like Mr. Williams, would we?"

"Who is he? What have you done to him, you freak?"

"Mr. Williams has serious problems accepting the truth that we are trying to feed him. We have shown him his movie hundreds and hundreds of times for several weeks, but he has proven to be strong and simply will not accept the treatment even when we showed him the charred bodies. It's all so sad."

"What about Angela?" Meredith spat out every single word.

"Ah, Angela! You like her, don't you? I remember when she came to us. A young woman full of life. She was much like yourself. Too curious for her own good and, sadly, she threatened to report me. I could not have that and after hundreds and hundreds of hours watching herself mutilating and slaughtering her poor boyfriend, she finally became a believer. Oh, Meredith! You should see them! That final moment right when they realize what they have done, and they start to see things our way. It's beautiful! And now that you know, you too will need treatment."

"No! You mustn't! You can't! Freak, monster, pervert!" Meredith screamed in rage while two guards held her down.

"Oh, Meredith, Meredith, why did you slaughter all those patients?"

Shed Skin

"911, how may I be of assistance?"

"It's my neighbor. She is acting unusually strange. Running around in the street screaming that her cat Spencer tried to kill her. She's all covered in blood, so something happened to her."

"I see. Do you know if your neighbor suffers from any mental illness? No drug abuse?"

"Not that I'm aware of."

"I see. I will send a car over to your address. Until it arrives I would advise you not to engage the woman in any way. Leave that to us."

"You got it."

Peter hung up the phone and went back to the kitchen window. It all seemed very strange. Ms. West was a nice lady who sat knitting every day on her front porch with her cat sleeping in her lap when Peter came home on his bike from work. She would wave at him, and he would stay and make small talk about the weather and other trivial things. Never in his life could he imagine her being an addict or mentally ill. She just looked too much like a nice old lady, a grandmother who would give you cookies and lemonade every time you stopped by but then again. There she was, running around in the streets wearing nothing but her nightgown, and stains of clear red blood pierced through the white fabric as she was begging for her life.

For a brief moment, Peter thought about going outside and helping the old lady back in her house but there was something deep inside Peter that told him to remain indoor. The police car finally arrived and two cops went out to talk to her. Peter stood close to one of the windows in the kitchen that was ajar in order to hear the conversation, but it was hard to make out any words. The woman appeared to be in a state of shock because as far as Peter heard she did not speak a word.

The two cops spoke to the old woman for quite a while and Peter admired their patience considering that the lady seemed to be completely unaware of their presence. Finally, they decided to bring her down to the station for further examination whereon the woman did something that would be imprinted in Peter's mind forever for in a matter of seconds the old woman had jumped the back on one of the cops and broken the young man's neck. After that, she jumped the other officer, forced him to the ground, and ripped his heart out.

Peter stood completely still, pale from what he had just witnessed, and reached for his phone to make a second 911 call but stayed his hand just as he had unlocked the screen. The old woman had started making strange, tormented noises whereon she started scratching her skin as if it pained her. Large chunks of flesh fell off her body and when she could not get it off by hand, she tore it off with her mouth and ate it.

Unable to control his reaction, Peter threw up right on the window causing a sound that attracted the attention of the creature and it fixed its eyes on Peter's house. Quickly, he dropped to the floor and prayed that the creature would walk away. In complete silence, he sat under the kitchen counter and held his phone in a tight grip. The woman or creature, or whatever it was, had stopped screaming, and not a sound could be heard. Peter took a deep breath and hoped for the best.

He started making his way out from the counter when he suddenly heard a window break. She had been waiting for him. Peter made a run for it and aimed for the bedroom further down the hall and he almost made it when he felt her hand grasping his ankle. It was cold and wet from all the blood and Peter started kicking her off. To his surprise, it was remarkably simple for she was very fragile and broke easily like a rotten piece of wood and he managed to come loose with nothing more than a scratch.

Exhausted from the attack, Peter went into the bedroom to rest for a while. There was a rank odor in the room that was hard to ignore but Peter felt that he had to at least catch his breath. He put his head on the pillow and felt nausea coming fast and instinctively he knew that something was horribly wrong.

"Ward! Ward! Where the hell are you?" The chief of police had the voice he always used when he needed something, and Ward had heard it all too often. With too much work on his hands, the chief of police had a tendency of forgetting that other people also had things to do. Ward had learned not to let it get to him and, therefore, he settled with a short "yes". It was perfect because it often seemed to have a calming effect on his boss as well.

"Ward, I need you to go and check something out. An hour ago, we received a call about a woman behaving suspiciously. We sent a car but there has been no radio contact for the last hour. You and Ash must go and check it."

"Sure, but I bet you it is a waste of time. I'm sure their radio is malfunctioning or something."

"Maybe, and, if so, I'll admit my mistake but please go see to them." Ward grabbed his coat and made a quick detour by an office where he knocked twice on the door. A young detective named Ashley opened the door. She was not really his partner but of all the detectives in the house, she was the one he respected the most, and by what could be a happy coincidence she just happened to be one of the few in the building who could stand working with him.

It was no more than a twenty-minute drive from the station, but Ward managed to squeeze in enough complaints to annoy Ashley to the point where she almost considered jumping out in full speed and take her chances. Ward was furious over the fact that he was forced to do what he referred to as beginner's work and no matter how Ashley tried to convince him to think positive, he just kept going on like a broken record.

After a ride that felt as if it had gone on for days and days, Ward and Ashley finally arrived at the neighborhood where they had lost connection with the other car. The actual car was not hard to find. It was blinking away in the middle of the street with both front doors open. Ward felt like he always did when he knew that something was wrong and this time he felt like something was horribly wrong.

"Grab your gun," he told Ashley.

"I think you might be right on that one," she quickly replied. The air was quiet as they left the car and moved forward.

"Hello? Is someone there?" Ward yelled out into the night but there was no answer. The squad car was empty and there was not a single sign from the two cops. All of a sudden, the silence was abruptly interrupted by a shriek so ghastly it could freeze the blood. Ward and Ashley ran to the house where the scream came from.

The door to the front porch was wide open and there were stains of dark red blood all over the porch as if something had bled its way into the house. As they entered the house, they were struck by a foul stench of flesh and Ashley instinctively knew that it was a bad idea to come here. As they entered the kitchen, they were faced with the mutilated bodies of the two officers who were missing. Ward gazed at the corpses and then he turned to Ashley.

"Slowly back out of here as quiet as you can and go to the car and call for backup. Do it now."

Ashley, still struggling with what she just witnessed, did not say anything but started backing with a tight grip around her gun and exited the house. As she left Ward, he heard a strange sound as if an animal was scratching the inside of the door further down the hallway. With silent steps, he moved toward the door and raised his gun while he reached to open the door with his other hand. No more had he turned the doorknob before something, like out of a person's worst nightmare, crashed through the wooden door and attacked him.

Ward held his arm up to try and fend the beast away while attempting to get a clear shot with his other arm. Suddenly, the horrid deformity bit his arm all the way through his jacket and on through his skin. The pain was agonizing but at least he could get a shot. He put the gun to the creature's temple and pulled the trigger. The thing fell dead to the floor and Ashley came running with her gun drawn.

"What happened? Are you okay?" She saw the dead thing and Ward tending his wounded arm.

"Go into the room and see what you can find," Ward said. Ashley ventured on into what appeared to be the bedroom.

"There is another dead body here and from what I can see that thing has taken huge chunks of it." She bent down to examine the body and picked out a wallet from the back pocket. "This guy's named Peter. Could be the one who called the police."

"It would appear so," Ward agreed. "Can we get back to the station? My arm hurts and I need a tetanus shot."

"Of course. I've called in backup. They can handle this," Ashley replied, and they hurried back to the station.

Ward's arm was still hurting but at least the wound had been properly cleaned and a nurse had put bandages on it. At the moment, Ward was happy just sitting at his office not doing anything. The struggle had left him tired and weary but most of all there was an odd feeling in his body. A hunger he could not seem to get rid of. He tried eating a sandwich, but it was like eating thin air and the hunger was still palpable and his stomach hurt badly. With nothing more to eat, he started to feel irritated and a wave of anger began to rise within him.

He tried to control himself and calm down, but it did not get better. The hunger was immense and now his entire body started itching as if a thousand ants feasted upon his very skin. In a kind of manic stage, he tried scratching himself all over but if anything, it made things worse.

Ward started breathing heavily and scratched his aching body more and more with a furious intensity until the skin suddenly cracked and fell to the floor. The sight was as bizarre as it was macabre and still, something was alluring about it. The way it lay there like a pudding, juicy and tender. Ward felt the hunger again and with a beastly intensity, he ate the entire skin of his body until there was nothing more left of him but naked muscles and tendons.

At first, the hunger was stilled, and Ward actually felt fed, but the feeling did not last very long and soon the cravings started coming back. They came like a rising tide and Ward felt a desire to eat. A need for more food, more flesh, and, like a predator on the prowl, he left the office in the hunt for fresh meat.

The carnage that followed was like a grotesque feast of blood and flesh and in nothing but a matter of minutes the entire police department was dead or dying. Ashley, who had been out to get some coffee, knew nothing of the massacre and as far as she knew all her coworkers and friends were still alive and well.

The bloodbath she witnessed when entering the station had her paralyzed with fear and in an obscene pile of perversion and mutilation, Ward stood, devouring a piece of meat. When he noticed that she was there, he abruptly stopped eating and stared with tiny furious eyes right at her.

Ashley froze and instinctively she tried to reach for her gun. Ward, whose hunger was only greater, began moving toward her. He did not speak any more but only gave away a kind of roaring sound as he advanced on his prey. Finally, Ashley was able to grab a hold of her gun and with a shaking hand, she raised it against him and emptied the clip. Ward fell backward twitching on the floor and after a while, his naked muscles relaxed as he died.

The rest of the day was horrible as the emergency center sent both police and military to investigate and clean up the mess. Ashley was questioned several times and it was not until late at night that she came home and was able to lie down on the couch. Her cat Edna was missing and could not be found. Suddenly, she came through an open window.

Apparently, she had been fighting with the neighborhood dog once again because she had a scratch mark on her left paw. Ashley took no bigger notice of this as the two of them always seemed to fight about something. She took the cat into the bathroom to clean her up but just as Ashley was about to put her in the bathtub Edna bit her and ran away. Ashley, being too tired to care, went back to the couch to get some rest and there she fell asleep.

When she woke up, there were tiny footprints of bloody paws all over the apartment and Ashley followed the tracks all the way to the closet. The door was half open and from inside she could hear moaning and groaning sounds as from a cat in pain. A sudden wave of unease came over Ashley as she had a feeling of what she would find once she opened the door.

Inside the dusky closet, a being born out of hell itself fixed its eyes right at her while making hissing sounds and waving its still furry tail. It was the police station all over again and Ashley cried out in sheer agony and desperation while the creature jumped and attacked her, ripping huge chunks of meat from her body.

Several hours later, Ashley woke up with a strange feeling. A terrible hunger she had never felt before. She got out of bed only to find that she could barely balance herself on her legs. Her eyesight was blurry and she struggled to find her way to the kitchen. There she helped herself to the leftovers of a grilled chicken. The meat felt good between her teeth and yet it would not satisfy her need. The meat simply felt too processed, too cooked, and when she had finished eating, she still felt famished.

Ashley wandered around the flat aimlessly. The cat was nowhere to be seen and there was no more meat in the apartment. She knew what was about to happen, she had seen it before. She lay herself down on the floor, waiting to turn into something most unnatural and with her last thought, she reached for her gun and two shots echoed in the night.

Across from Ashley's flat, in the next building, Randy sat at his kitchen table like he usually did. He had retired from his job as a bus driver a long time ago and enjoyed the quiet life with his wife and dog Theo. Randy was a man of habits and preferred if most of the days were alike. After breakfast, he would take Theo out for a walk and then once again in the afternoon just before the three o'clock news.

This day, however, was not an ordinary day. His wife, Brenda, had gone out to buy the paper and a couple of donuts. This would normally take her about twenty minutes, thirty if it was crowded, but when she had been gone for almost an hour, Randy began to worry. After all, she was old and needed a walking stick to keep her from falling.

Randy turned on the radio to listen if there had been any major accidents, but the radio mentioned nothing about that. Suddenly, Brenda opened the door and walked inside. Randy immediately noticed that her cane was missing and there was something stressed in her eyes as if she was a hunted animal.

"Where on earth have you been?" he asked.

"Shh! Quiet, you!" She slammed and locked the door behind her and stood still listening carefully. It was quiet. The only thing to be heard was Theo who was wagging his tail as always. Randy was beginning to get even more worried for he had never seen his wife like this before. She was truly frightened. Suddenly, she took a deep breath and fell on the chair next to the door. "Finally!" she said to herself.

"My dear Brenda, please tell me what has happened. You're pale as if a ghost chased you here."

"I wish it was a ghost but no. This was no ghost. I was on my way to buy the paper when all of a sudden something horrid came right at me. I was so scared. It just lashed right at me as if it was trying to eat me."

"Eat you? What the hell are you talking about? Was it a hobo?"

"No, nothing like that. I don't know. It is hard to describe. I tried not to look at it but I can tell you this. It was like nothing out of this world. Like a hell hound spawned onto earth." Brenda's eyes were wide and full of fear as if what she had seen would leave a deep scar within her soul forever.

"I'm so glad that you made it back here alive. Come here and let me hug you," Randy said. Brenda got herself off the chair but instantly fell back down in pain. Randy carefully lifted the lower part of her skirt, revealing a big scratch mark.

"The thing must have scratched me without me knowing it." The marks were deep and dark red blood was slowly pumped out from the wound.

"We have to get you to a hospital, my dear," Randy said. "I'm going to put a bandage over it for now." He went to get the bandages while Brenda sat at the chair. She rarely got hungry but this experience had triggered her hunger. She gazed down at the wound. It was still pumping out blood. Sweet, delicious blood. Just a little sip of that blood would be refreshing for her and give her the energy back. She was surprised and abhorred by her own thoughts and yet she could not stop herself. Like a moth drawn to the flame, she began licking the blood, sucking it in like a lovely treat.

Randy was still out in the kitchen looking for the first aid kit. It took some time since it was on the top shelf in the cabinet and he simply was not as nimble as he used to be. Out in the hallway, Brenda had licked the wound perfectly clean but despite all the blood she had drunk, her lust for that sweet taste of iron still could not be slaked; and with a furious rage, she started tearing the flesh of her body feasting upon it like steaks. The skin came off easily and when Randy finally came back, half of her skin was missing and hung like it was about to fall off.

When Brenda saw her husband, she suddenly stopped eating, turned her head, and glared right at him. Randy was so startled that he jumped back instinctively. The thing that once was his true love hissed at him and started moving in his direction. All of a sudden, Theo walked into the hall from having slept in the bed. When Brenda saw the dog, she fixed her eyes upon the poor dog which looked back at her with wide-open uncomprehending eyes. Brenda started crawling on all four toward the animal.

In a pure panic, Randy tried to grab hold of something to defend Theo with and after having fumbled around, he finally came across the meat cleaver. Without further thought, he stepped in between Brenda and Theo and raised the weapon against her. The thing hissed at Randy in an attempt to threaten him, but Randy stood his ground and struck down upon the thing. The meat cleaver hit between its eyes.

The blood of his wife stained his face and without a single word or expression Randy went to the kitchen table, poured himself a cup of coffee, and turned on the radio. In the apartment, the voice of the radio host echoed speaking of a new plague spreading across the earth.

Earlier the same day, Bud was sitting in a corner of a street. It was a slow day in spite of the nice weather. He looked down at the bottom of his cup. One, fifty. On a good day, he could have up to six bucks in there or even more. This, however, was a bad time of the month. It was too far from the last payday and too close to the next one and people held on to the final coins of their salary to make it to the next.

Bud did not blame them. He would probably have done the same thing. He had done the same thing way back when he had a job. In the days when he had been one of those who walked past without dropping anything in the cup.

He grew tired of sitting on the ice-cold pavement for nothing but nickels and dimes and he put the cup down to take his one fifty and buy himself a hot cup of coffee. Bud got himself up and was just about to go to the gas station across the street when he heard a strange noise from one of the dumpsters in the alley behind him.

Bud was torn. On the one hand, he felt like he really should check out what that odd sound was but, on the other hand, he had a little something called survival instinct and for some reason, he felt that whatever was in that dumpster was evil. He could not explain why but it was as if the whole alley reeked of death.

Finally, he decided to take a look. If it turned out to be a corpse or anything like that, he would leave the place and make an anonymous phone call to the police. Bud knew he was at the bottom of society and he also knew what the police thought about his kind on a crime scene.

The sight that met Bud as he opened the dumpster stretched his mind to the very brink of madness for inside was a throng of rat-like creatures but they were only like rats in the shape of their bodies for their fur was gone and now they had the appearance of the unholy offspring of the devil himself.

Suddenly, one of the abominations made a jump at Bud and bit him in the neck. Bud threw the thing away and the smell of a bloody rat seemed to attract predators because from nowhere came a cat and attacked the thing. It was an unfair fight which the cat easily won with nothing more than a scratch. From a distance, Bud could hear someone calling out to the cat, "Spencer, Spencer! Where are you?" The cat made a nimble jump and disappeared to one of the houses in the next block.

Bud fell to his knees in pain. He felt hungry and craved nothing more than to eat meat. Fresh, juicy meat.

Bodies

I

Let me start by saying that I have always considered myself a man of science. I believe only in what I can prove, and I consider Darwin's theories fact. The only thing I have ever trusted are my two own eyes and what they can see. I have spent most of my life studying genetic abnormalities in animals trying to find an answer as to how it is that certain species manage to adapt to environments normally lethal to them. However, none of these teachings can even come close to describe what I have witnessed.

It all started when an old friend of mine, Dr. Wall, called me and asked me to consult him about a matter of most urgency. Dr. Wall is an archaeologist and I wondered what he might have found that could possibly be of interest to someone that studies animals. I was curious as to how I could be of any assistance, and I asked him over the phone, but he refused to speak of the matter and instead he insisted that I would join him as soon as possible.

As it was, I took the very next flight down to the excavation site in the southern U.S.A. From there, I had to take the boat to a remote island far from the coastline in the middle of the ocean. It was a hot day and I remember that I thought it was a strange place for an excavation. The island was nothing more than razor-sharp rocks and dead vegetation. Not much to dig in and even less possible to find any bones since I doubt that many animals would find their way out here. The only thing alive on the island as far as I could see apart from us, was a couple of seagulls circling the sea for fish.

Although I could not quite explain what it was, there was something about the place which made me feel uneasy. It was as if the very air seemed thicker around the island and a strong feeling began to grow inside my body telling me that we should not be here. Despite my feelings, I could not push myself to tell the others since it was only something in my head but the entire walk from the tiny beach to the site, I was filled with agony as I started to regret ever agreeing to the trip in the first place.

When we finally came to the place where they had set up camp, I could not help but notice the weary looks upon the faces of the workers. It was as if they too felt the unwelcoming presence telling us to leave. It was clearer in their eyes since they had been on the island far longer than I. Troubled by what I saw, I felt that I needed answers, but I decided to let it go for the moment and instead find my friend. The good doctor waited for me in a tent a little further away and I was hoping that he would provide me with some answers to the workers' health, but instead, I found him to be in a worse state than any of the others.

"Is it really that bad?" he asked me and forced a smile to his lips. "It is good to see you, my friend. I can tell from the look on your face that you have seen the state of all of us." I nodded carefully and could not help but notice his eyes. They were gloomy and appeared to have lost much of their former bright color and were now gray, like mist on a late November day.

"It is the fumes of this place," he said, coughing from his lungs. "Mankind was never meant to set foot here, I can tell you that much." I gazed upon his ghostlike figure and shuddered. "There are caves on this island," he continued. "Caves that go deeper than any other places on earth and they spit out poisonous gas lethal to man when inhaled for too long. My men and I did not know this when we decided to venture here. We have been here for only two weeks and already you can see the effects on us."

"Why did you send for me?" I had to ask him and I am sure he could detect the irritation in my voice as I heard it myself.

"I did not drag you all the way out here just to get you ill if that is what you are implying," he quickly remarked. "There is something I have to show you. Something remarkable." For the first time since I got here, I could see a sparkle in his eyes, and he immediately got me intrigued.

I followed him outside and he took me to one of the caves that they had been examining. "We have to go down," he told me. "Put on a protective suit, or your skin will corrode in contact with the underground water." I dressed up in a suit that looked like something caught from a movie and we were lowered down into one of the biggest pits.

I am not an expert on caves or types of rocks but some of the stones we saw on our way down were kinds I have never seen in my entire life and I am pretty certain they only existed on that very island. The bottom of the cave was magnificent, to say the least. The main room where they had set up the research center was a vast cave that seemed to run mile after mile into the mountain.

"This is the biggest cave we have discovered so far," Wall explained to me. "There appear to be several more but we dare not venture any further. Follow me. We are going to one of the smaller ones adjacent to this."

I felt like a little boy as I walked around in uncharted territory looking for treasure and, for a moment, I knew what it must be like to be an astronaut. Words cannot describe the humbleness I felt as I wandered the caves. We came to a narrow tunnel and Wall signaled me to follow him. It was a long way to go with those suits and it got even smaller as we got closer. By the end of the tunnel, it was so narrow that I had to squeeze myself into the next room and I must admit that a feeling of claustrophobia started to rise within me.

The sight that met me in the room had me stunned and I froze in wonder of what was before me. A giant hall filled with the most detailed murals I have ever seen. They seemed to be done in such a careful way that I remember thinking that no man could ever have done them. Yet, there was something odd and most disturbing about them, for as I looked closer, I noticed that the things they depicted were obscene and perverse images of ancient rituals.

"The devil's work, right?" I suddenly heard Wall behind me say. I had been so busy studying the murals that I had forgotten he was there.

"How is this possible?" I asked with great surprise.

"You tell me. Not even animals live on this island. The environment is too rough for them, but this is not all." We went on a bit further into the cave and, once again, I became dizzy with admiration and a great shiver ran down my spine, for, now, we stood right in the middle of what appeared to be an ancient burial chamber. I say "appear" since I have never seen a tomb like this before. Every carcass was neatly hanged from the ceiling upside down with their throats carefully cut in order to drain them of blood. Someone had then stitched the wounds back together with great precision. The fumes of the place had preserved the bodies in a stage much like mummification. All of the bodies, I should add, were humanoid as far as I could tell, and they appeared to have been quite young when it happened.

"It is strange," Wall said. "Their bodies should be completely corroded by the fumes but instead it preserved them perfectly. This is why I wanted you here. It would seem like these creatures, these... humans" – the words did not come easy to him – "somehow adapted to this hostile place. Look at this." He pointed to a corner in the cave I had failed to see.

All of a sudden it became obvious why they had hanged their dead upside down because in front of me now was a grotesque altar filled with the most well-made vials of liquid. It did not require any further research to guess what was in those vials. It was not uncommon for tribes to do this as there are several examples where people believe that a person's soul lives on in their blood.

"Some form of heathen tradition," Wall mumbled, "but that is not the strange part. Take a look inside the vial." I reached out to a vial and peeked inside expecting to see regular, coagulated blood. However, this blood was not coagulated at all but fresh and it had an odd discoloring to it that gave it almost a yellow-brown shade. I was baffled by this great discovery and immediately asked that Wall and his men would allow me to bring the bodies back to the university along with the vials for closer examination.

Wall was not hard to persuade and I got the feeling that he had expected me to make that request. The rest of his men were very glad to help me load the findings as it meant getting off this godforsaken island. The very next day everything was loaded and we were ready to leave for civilization. The mood on the boat back to shore was slightly better but I could tell that the crew was uneasy about the cargo, and it was not until my plane had left with the carcasses that they felt safe again. I promised Dr. Wall that I would be in touch with him as soon as I had some answers.

II

On my flight home, I could not focus my mind on anything else than what I had just seen. It was a weird reality to be faced with and though the cargo frightened me down to my very soul, there was something deep inside me that had me fascinated with these beings. Just the idea that they, of all people on earth, had found a way to adapt to the unfriendly environment on that island had me intrigued. Such a discovery would throw my research years, no decades, into the future.

Back at the university, I asked one of the assistants to help organize the boxes from the plane. I also had her catalog all of the vials and put them in a locked storage room so that there would be no accidents. I had taken several pictures of the murals found on the walls of the cave and I started by having them processed so I could start examining them.

While I waited for the pictures, I started lining up all the bodies carefully so that I could perform an autopsy. It was a strange feeling to be standing among findings that could lead to a Nobel Prize and it was with the humblest feeling that I began cutting one of the tribe members open. As a man of science, I expected to find dried entrails but what I saw when I opened the body had me stunned in a terrible shock. The sweat poured from my forehead and I felt a severe increase of stress as my pulse rushed tremendously. Quickly, I ran over to some of the other bodies and cracked them open but what I found had me so weak that I fell to my knees and one of the assistants had to aid me to a chair.

"Bring me the phone…" I asked of her quietly.

"Is there something wrong?"

"Bring me the phone! The phone I said! Now!" The poor woman looked at me as if I had gone mad but brought me the phone nonetheless. As soon as I had it in my lap, I called up Wall.

"Wall speaking."

"Wall… the bodies… they…" I struggled to find words.

"Who is this? Alfred, is that you?"

I took a couple of deep breaths and tried again. "These bodies, the bodies we found that I brought… they are not ancient, not ancient at all."

"Wait a minute. What are you telling me here?"

"Wall, I have performed many autopsies in my days, and I tell you, these carcasses are no more than a couple of hundred years old."

"What the hell are you saying?"

"These people died in the early nineteenth century." There was a profound silence that lasted for several minutes. After a while, it felt like time had stopped and we just sat there waiting for one of us to say something.

"How can this be?" Wall suddenly asked. "Those bodies were dried like raisins."

"I know but looking at their intestines makes me certain. They are not old. Come here tomorrow and I will show you."

That night, sleep eluded me as I lay pondering any explanation that would make at least some sense, but none came to mind. After many hours, when the sun was coming back up, I finally fell asleep from sheer exhaustion. I dreamed of disturbing rituals of perversion and twisted fantasies including body fluids and brutal slaughter. Abruptly, I woke up and stared into the bland wallpaper in front of me for a long time, sweating like an anxious pig being brought to the butcher. There was something sinister going on, I just knew it.

In the car on my way to work, I got stuck in a traffic jam and without noticing it, my car was right outside a graveyard. I sat there in the hot car staring out over the bleak view. *Why did we do it? Why were we there in the first place?* Suddenly, I realized that I had not asked myself these questions. *How did Wall and his men even know where to start looking?* I needed to find out more about the expedition before it was too late.

When I got to the university, Wall was already waiting for me at the parking lot. As soon as we entered the building, I got a bad feeling. I could not put my finger on it but I knew that there was trouble ahead. When we came to the hall where I kept the findings, we were both devastated for someone had broken in and destroyed everything. The bodies were desecrated and the vials empty and broken on the floor. I panicked and begun picking up the pieces of the broken vials from the floor. Wall, on the other hand, was paralyzed and gazed out across the mess chanting "No, no, no" to himself over and over again.

After a while, the police came to investigate but no evidence was to be found and the tape from the surveillance camera was missing. Over the next following days, Wall locked himself inside his room and refused to speak to anyone. I began feeling bad that I had doubted the good doctor and after he had spent a couple of days in isolation, I decided to force myself into his room. The knocking had no effect as he would not even dignify me with an answer so, with no other option, I broke down the door only to find him over me with a knife.

"I… I am sorry," he said with a far-off expression on his face. "I thought you were someone else."

"Who?" I snapped back at him. The room was dark and up until now, I had not seen his face, but, now, he responded to me by turning toward me with a smug grin and I could see that his eyes had turned gray again.

"Wall?" I asked him when both of us had calmed down a bit.

"Yes?"

"How did you actually come to know about that island?"

Wall gazed out into thin air for a while, then he said with a tone of surprise, "You know what? It is kind of funny. I do not remember. It was like something I just had to do. Like a vision… a dream… telling me to go there." He became absent and I decided not to push him any further.

III

Although every inch of my body told me to leave things alone while I was still sane, I felt that I needed to do something to help my friend as he was clearly ill. I studied every single thing from the excavation site once again without any positive results. Then I examined the photos taken from within the cave where the bodies were found. Most of it was just sheer perversion and depicted sexual rites too graphic to even imagine but one of the murals depicted something entirely different. I shivered in fear of the mere sight of the mural. Young men drinking the body fluids of their elder tribe members who were hung upside down just like in the cave. If this was some heathen ritual, it was repulsive and yet I could not help but think that it was connected with the recent events in the morgue.

Meanwhile, I got reports that several of the members of the expedition had been forced to seek help at a hospital due to a sudden decline in their health. When I began asking around, all of them had the same symptoms. Loss of sight and a rising fever. I telephoned Wall to see how he was doing but had a hard time making out anything he said. When I got there, he was in a terrible state. His body looked completely dehydrated and he was sweating uncontrollably. His sight had been so heavily damaged that I had to stand right in front of my friend for him to even see me.

I called an ambulance and he was rushed to the hospital where the other crew members were being treated. The doctors, however, had no reasonable explanation and when I came to visit Wall at the hospital a few days later, he looked as if he had been purged of all his life force. The muscles in his body had been atrophied and he was now completely blind.

Determined to find answers as to what had caused the illness, I went to Wall's room in search of clues. At first, I found nothing but, then, stuffed inside his pillowcase, I found the lost surveillance tape. The things I saw on the tape had me question my own eyes for I saw Wall and his men break into the morgue and swallow the body fluids of the old mummies as if it was nothing.

While I was still coping with what I had just witnessed, they called me from the hospital to inform me that all of the crew members including Wall had passed away right around the same time. The doctors claimed that the cause of death was extreme malnutrition but I knew that was only one part of the truth. I ordered the hospital to give me a sample of blood from one of the bodies. They agreed and I hurried there as fast as I could.

As soon as I set foot at the hospital, I could tell that they had made the discovery I expected them to make. One of the doctors came up to me with a face so pale that he looked as if he had seen a ghost and, in total silence, he handed over the blood and it had the same yellow-brown shade I had seen inside the cave and not very surprisingly, it was fresh as if the bodies still were alive. I saw that the young doctor in front of me anxiously was awaiting a reasonable explanation but since I had none to give, I just took the sample and left.

Back at my laboratory, I took some of the blood and put it under a microscope. What I discovered is easy to explain but almost impossible to accept for in the blood were millions of parasites that seemed to be living of the blood and reshaping it into a different organism just like mutation. It is impossible for me to explain it any better than that as I have never seen anything like it. Seconds after I got a phone call from the hospital. It was the young doctor who had given me the blood.

"The bodies... Oh, God... The bodies... The bodies are alive!"

Darkness

Then the Lord said to Moses, "Stretch out your hand toward the sky so that darkness will spread over Egypt – darkness that can be felt." So Moses stretched out his hand toward the sky, and total darkness covered all Egypt for three days. No one could see anyone else or leave his place for three days.
Exodus 10:21–23

I

It was simply one of those regular nights. People came home from their jobs, young people left school for the week and everywhere the people made themselves ready for the weekend. It was a Friday in late October and the news reported nothing out of the ordinary. I, myself, finished work at four o'clock and was on my way home after a long week I most preferably could have been spared. Now I just longed for a beer in my hand in front of some half-bad movie that I could fall asleep to.

Other people look forward to the weekends because it gives them a chance to go out and be social, but I have never enjoyed working with the people around me and I simply do not care for the environment in nightclubs.

There is something about being forced to be so close to so many people that just makes me feel stressed and nauseated. I would not go so far as to call myself antisocial, I'm just not thrilled about the idea of socializing with people. Fortunately, I'm married to a woman who understands me and does not push me to do things I do not want to do. Our house is at the edge of the town, a few miles away from the city and if I go out in the yard, I see nothing but trees.

Friday evening proceeded without any warning signs that something would be wrong. I fell asleep as usual on the sofa and Vanessa, my wife, went to bed without waking me up. Much later that night, I woke up and waddled off to the bedroom to sleep the remaining hours of the night. I still remember thinking that I could not have slept very long on the couch because it was still dark outside. Without putting more emphasis on it, I slept on.

Since it was Saturday and I had a free weekend, I took the opportunity to sleep longer and I did not bother to set the alarm clock. Therefore, I was not sure what time it was when I finally woke up and discovered that it was still dark outside. Drowsy and confused, I began to fumble for the alarm clock that I knew was on the nightstand. According to the clock, it was already nine o'clock and as soon as I woke up a little more, I noticed that Vanessa had gone up so I pulled on a pair of pants and a shirt that was at the side of the bed and followed to see what was going on.

The whole house was dark except for a few lights in the windows that we rarely put out and outside it was dark as if it was in the middle of the night. Confused, I shouted at Vanessa, but no one answered. Then I went downstairs and found that the front door was wide open and further out on the stairs Vanessa stood in her nightgown, staring toward heaven as if she was paralyzed. I went to her and tried to make contact but she stood absolutely still as if someone had petrified her, staring almost manically at the sky. I have to admit that I lost my breath when I went outside the door to find it so dark that nothing was visible past the gate posts.

It was like a bizarre dream, and my first thought was that there had to be something wrong with the clocks and that it was still night, but according to all the clocks that we looked at, it was early morning. There was no sign that it would turn lighter and there seemed to be no reasonable explanation for the phenomenon. It was as if the whole world soaked in total darkness with no hope of morning.

Hoping to get answers to what was happening, we turned on the T.V. and sat in the dark. No matter which channel we chose it was the same news. The news, however, gave no answers as to what happened, and the main message was to not panic but just take it easy and wait for further instructions.

That message went like a dull jingle all day, and, to some extent, it worked on the masses. People want to hear that all is well and that there is nothing to be afraid of. It is one of those basic needs we all have left since childhood when our mothers told us that there was nothing in the dark closet to fear. People can relax, if only for a little while, and feel that someone else will take care of their problems.

We made it through the first day. We had a bit more lights lit than usual and made sure to stay inside as much as we could. After a while, it ended up in what I can best describe as denial or perhaps forgetfulness, and the mind managed to convince itself that it was probably a natural phenomenon that would soon pass. We almost succeeded in persuading ourselves that we imagined it all, or maybe that it would go away by itself.

The night was like any night, and we went to bed with an imaginary sense of security and that everything would be as usual when we woke up. The night seemed strangely long and I slept very restlessly. I guess most did. Everyone was waiting for it to be morning. A long-awaited morning when you could breathe out. I was lying and listened to the steady ticking of the alarm clock that did not hurry the slightest. The closer it was to morning, the more it started to feel like when you were a child and knew that it was your birthday the following day. The stomach tingled and I had a feeling I have not had in many years. Eventually, however, I fell asleep for a few hours.

When the alarm clock rang (this time I had set the alarm at eight), I woke up and went straight to the window and pulled up the blinds. The feeling that struck me was like a fist straight in the stomach. It was, if possible, even darker and from the window, I could not even see the garden. As in panic, I ran out on the lawn, and I could almost feel the darkness pressing on and creating a most disturbing feeling in my body. Vanessa was just behind me out, and her reaction was more direct and full of despair. She walked around the lawn barefoot even though it was almost freezing cold and chanted "no, no, no" to herself without showing signs of being remotely able to communicate.

Finally, I managed to get her in and sit on the couch with me to see what the T.V. had to say about all this. It proved to be the same news anchors as the day before, and now they only told us that they still had not received any response, but scientists were examining the matter and they urged people to stay calm. This time, however, the words did not have the effect they desired, and one after another reports of traffic chaos and accidents began to come in. Vanessa slowly turned toward me, and her eyes stared at me in terror as if she had met her maker.

"You have to go in and buy food and supplies. Now." The tone of her voice told me that it was not open for discussion, and somewhere inside me, I knew she was right, even if I did not feel like mixing with so many people and especially people who were scared and stressed. Suddenly, I felt pressure in me building up a solid brick wall that I could not get over. I took a few deep breaths and got ready to tell Vanessa that I could not do this, but at the same moment that I turned my head toward her, I saw a horror far deeper than the one I felt, and slowly I began to understand that I had to do this.

II

I do not think that a drive has ever taken so long as it did now. For every kilometer closer I got to the store, the worse I felt. The darkness was heavy around the car as thick soot and headlights helped only marginally. As I approached the supermarket, it became apparent to me that my worst fears had come true. The parking lot was crowded with cars and in total desperation, people had continued to park up on the lawn and all the other places where you could possibly fit a car.

Almost instinctively, my breathing became shallower and I had to take a few minutes to myself and calm down my nerves before I went in. Eventually, I decided to overcome my fear and just do what I had to do. In my hand, I kept a list of things that needed to be purchased, and right now this was the only thing that made me feel secure. Knowing that I had something where I could check off one thing after another made it all feel a little easier.

The weak sense of relief I just felt disappeared abruptly, however, when the glass doors to the store opened and I saw the chaos that has broken out in the shop. People dragged around large boxes of tin cans and water bottles and thronged to the shelves just for the chance to get the last oil lamp. Sales assistants ran up and down the lanes like lab rats struggling to fill the shelves. I took a firm grip on the cart handle and went into the chaos.

It's hard to describe but I can best describe it as a horrible cacophony of tormented souls who climbed on each other like snakes in a pit. Some had unwisely chosen to bring their children to the store as if they thought it would be like any day now and these children, trapped in a shopping cart, cried loudly in agony. I really felt with them and felt like doing the same. Although no one knew what was happening out there, people knew that they would not sit without supplies.

I hastened to more or less throw the things I needed or even thought I might need. There was no margin to forget anything because it was not possible to reverse or even back when the whole supermarket was like one long winding queue until the end. The queue was moving far too slowly for me to feel comfortable and when it had gone far too long and I realized that I was only halfway. I began to have serious difficulty breathing and it was only then I noticed that I was standing right in the wine department. Without making a big deal of it, I took a bottle of red, turned the screw cap, and then I emptied half the contents.

The wine had a direct impact on my stress level, and I felt my nerves and muscles relax. It was not until that moment I realized how hard I had held on to the cart for once I relaxed as I discovered that my palms were bright red and the joints of the fingers so stiff that I could barely stretch them out properly. Then I realized that my so discreet action was not as discreet as I believed because a little further away there was a shop assistant looking very thoughtfully at me. A lump formed quickly in my stomach when I thought he would take me to a room where I had to explain myself, forcing me to stay even longer. Gently, I tried to read his intentions, but he must have understood how I felt because he let me be and returned to fill the shelves with canned fruits and looked no more in my direction.

I do not think I've ever been so happy to arrive at the checkout, and a little further away lay the pearly gates, also called the exit, which I would soon pass through. The car park was, if possible, even more crowded and it was full of angry and irritated people who could not get their cars out or had had their doors dented by others who had left without caring about what they hit. It was not hard to figure out that it was a matter of time before people started to run down each other if someone stood in the way. I found a shortcut over a hill and managed to exit to a smaller bike path and out on the road.

Traffic jams were endless, and the radio seemed to never stop reporting about traffic accidents and deaths. Everything was rapidly going from bad to worse, and no one could still give any explanation for the darkness that now lay so thick that it no longer mattered if the lights were on or not. I saw it as a minor miracle that I managed to get home. When I turned the key in the ignition to turn off the car, I was struck by a strange feeling that this could be the last time I saw the town.

III

The next few weeks the tone on radio and television became what can best be described as apocalyptic. First, consumption of happy pills and drugs drastically increased since people began to self-medicate in desperate attempts to repress the darkness around them. I certainly understand why they did it. It was a perfect human reaction to get the day to pass without committing suicide.

By now, they had stopped talking about days and nights as distinct concepts and instead talked about eternal night. The concept stuck in people and had an equally depressing connotation as it was dire. After a while, people even began to adapt their lives after the darkness. For a while, it felt like everything was finally about to stabilize. That was when everything started to go really wrong.

I know it sounds unlikely, but it was just like darkness felt that we adapted ourselves for suddenly the darkness took a new shape and turned into something no one had ever seen before. It was like tiny microscopic particles of soot that pushed their way in everywhere. If you got it on you the soot formed a fine powder that was extremely difficult to wash away and if you breathed it in you suffered a nasty dry cough that was extremely difficult to get rid of. On T.V. they said that they had investigated the particles and concluded that they were harmless. I've always been hesitant when someone vouches that something is "completely safe". That is usually when you should start running. This time, however, I had happily been wrong.

At first, it did not affect us much except that people seemed to be more irritable than usual. The number of assaults increased and spread an intimidating atmosphere in society that made it no longer safe to be outside alone. Then came the fires. Everywhere people lit everything on fire that could possibly burn. Entire car parks were burning and stores were stripped of goods and were then left to burn to the ground. The whole society was becoming a lawless country where the law of the jungle was the only law still in force. The police decided to take action and began to arm themselves heavily. The idea was that it would have a calming effect on the people, but it failed. That night when the riots broke out, it was cold outside, and the snow had begun to fall to the ground. The whole world felt like a big powder keg, and everyone was waiting for someone to give an excuse to pull out of personal war. The riots were something never seen before. All the people went from house to house to fight. Lawyers, engineers, and factory workers. Everyone wanted to be involved and to crack the skull of a fellow citizen.

The first ones to go were the pensioners who had the misfortune to be in the vicinity. Their bones were soft and they made little resistance. It was not so much "riots" as it was human slaughter and the police responded by shooting at the mass of souls who tore each other's limbs like wild animals. None, however, was on someone else's side, but all fought for the sake of violence. Television and radio were trying to report as long as possible, but, eventually, they also began to get carried away and the last thing viewers saw was a reporter who made an effort to drill through another man's head with a camera tripod.

The riots lasted seven whole days and when they were over, no one dared to say anything about the incident. We, who had the sense to barricade ourselves in our homes and did not expose ourselves to the darkness, could do nothing more than to just sit and wait for nothing. No reports came in and you could not even imagine how the city looked. There was a silence over the world as if no air were left to breathe. No one knew how many people had died little less how many were still alive.

It was then when no one thought it could get worse the storm came. It moved around the particles in the air, worse than ever, and pushed them into our homes. Parents killed their children, the children cut down their parents, and everyone was like starving predators in search of food. I had succeeded in finding two gas masks that were left after we renovated the house. I and Vanessa got them on in good time and they seemed to actually protect against the darkness. Vanessa hid in the basement and I had to bring all the food we had in the house down. Maybe it was because I lost the sense of how long we had actually been there, but, now, I discovered how little food we had left. The last time I went shopping, we thought the disaster would blow over in a week or so and that we could return to our normal lives.

When I told Vanessa that I had to go and try to pick what food now remained, she wept and so did I. I had felt uncomfortable about going the last time and that was nothing compared to what I felt now. Just the thought of having to go into the city made me feel bad. I managed to force myself and convinced myself that I had no choice. It was true. I had no choice, so I went out to the car and started rolling.

The sight that struck me when I approached the city made me shiver through my entire body, and though I was still in the suburban area, large parts of the town were either on fire or burned down. It was a barren land where no one lived. The darkness made it almost hopeless to see anything, but when I went into the city, the streets began to feel like a hilly path. Without thinking, I cranked down the window so that I could hear the sound of the surroundings. Unfortunately, I did not see my mistake until it was too late and a stench of ammonia and raw meat hit me, so that I had to quickly open the door and vomit. It was now that I realized that I was driving around on a former battlefield where the battle had now transformed the entire neighborhood into an open mass grave where bodies were stacked like simple garbage on a dump.

When I had gone a few hundred meters, I came to a supermarket and I drove up as close as I could get to avoid having to walk a lot. I threw the door open and rushed in as soon as I could but just when I would take the last step, I got caught with my foot in someone and fell into a puddle of half-coagulated blood. The foot was covered in what I can only believe bones and other things I don't even want to think about. The breathing became shallow and I now more or less gasped as if I was about to get a panic attack. Quickly, I grabbed hold of one of the shelves just above me and pushed myself up on my feet. When I finally managed to calm myself somewhat, my eyes started searching for supplies. It was not hard, it turned out almost all the shelves were full of food although there were clear signs of fighting even inside the store. It was as if the people had killed each other without showing the slightest interest in food.

I took two bags and filled them with as many canned goods as I could carry and ran out to the car again and just when it seemed that I would make it all the way, I heard a roar from across the street a little further away. The screams did not even sound human any more, but the tone had now shifted to an animal cry and it was almost impossible to make out words or letters. The only word I understood was "chasing" which cut through the masses like a blunt knife. I stepped on the gas and forced myself through the streets of corpses until I came to the outskirts of the city. Still, I could hear them running around in the streets like wild dogs in search of food, and I hurried home, hoping that Vanessa would be unharmed.

Immediately when I got inside, I barricaded the door and then I hurried down into the basement with the supplies. The basement was dark and it was too quiet for it to feel good. I called out for Vanessa, but no one answered. Despite the fear of what I would find if I turned on the light, I felt compelled to look. When I lit, I saw that it was empty, and the thoughts went directly to what could have happened. There was no blood or traces of her. I went further in and stood in the middle of the room. Then I saw something black in one corner and I went up to see what it was. It proved to be the gas mask that she for some reason had taken off. Immediately, my blood froze to ice, and I heard the ominous wind beat against the house. It was a miracle if no particles had penetrated the basement.

Suddenly, I had an uncomfortable feeling in my entire body as if I was not alone in the room. I saw no one and there was not a sound but there was something. As if someone was watching me from somewhere. A horrible bang was heard from outside and everything went black. I quickly realized that lightning must have struck nearby and I started fumbling for a flashlight. The next moment someone jumped up and attacked me in manic rage. Hands tore and clawed at my face, and I heard the growling sound of an angry dog. Somehow, I managed to throw off the attacker and flung out an arm in hope of finding a weapon. First, I found nothing but then my hand landed on a crowbar that stood in a corner. In pure instinct, I hit it until the growl ceased and the room turned silent once again. For a long time, I stood panting before I regained composure and managed to turn on a flashlight.

The sight when I lit the lamp was too horrid to imagine and I felt terrible nausea. It was Vanessa, or at least the remains of her. Now it looked more like a pile of meat and I fell down crying. No more than an hour later or so, morning came like the most natural thing in the world. As if it had never been gone.

My Own Mental Mansion

Theo woke up abruptly and grasped the duvet firmly as he sat up straight gasping for air violently. The reaction was so fierce it also awoke his wife who lay next to him.

"What the hell is going on?" she yelled to him in a voice far angrier than she intended.

"It's the same dream again. The same bloody dream and that damned house again."

"What house? What are you talking about? Honey, you had a bad dream, it's over now so go back to sleep." She tried to hide the irritation in her voice and the fact that he had woken her up after an already bad night. The kids had made them get water, follow them to the potty and finally lie beside them as they fell asleep again. Carla, Theo's wife, had not gotten any private sleeping time until midnight and now she was awake again. To tell the truth, she felt as if she had not slept an entire night ever since the kids were born. She let go of that thought and did her best to go back to sleep.

Theo however could not get any sleep. He stared into the wooden ceiling, his mind completely preoccupied with the house. It had returned to his dreams once more. It was really more of a mansion than a house and every time he dreamed about it, he got a feeling that he had actually been there at some point. He tried to remember but could not for the life of him recall ever visiting such a place.

He thought about the exterior of the mansion, the surroundings, he could even describe the interior in a frightening detailed way. The whole thing was a dream and yet not as something about it felt far real. Theo could not quite put his finger on it but there was a growing feeling within him that made Theo sure that the mansion actually existed.

The rest of the night, sleep eluded Theo and he welcomed the first rays of sunlight peeking in through the bedroom window. Just the fact that morning was nearly upon him felt comforting somehow. He went straight out of bed and out on the patio to get fresh air. Theo sat there for almost an hour before Carla awakened.

"Wow! You're up early! Not even the kids are awake yet," she remarked.

"Yeah, I know. I had a bad dream."

"Oh yes, I remember! About a house, right?"

"It's not just a house," Theo pointed out. "I've had dreams about this house several times and they keep coming back and it scares me."

"Gee, how bad can a house be? Is it our house?"

"No, it's not our house. This is larger, like a mansion and more…" Theo struggled to find words. "…more sinister. I think I've actually been there, or at least it feels like it."

"Well, can you describe it to me?"

"Of course, I can. I can describe it so well; it could be my childhood home. There are some stairs and a hall and…" Theo became silent for a moment. "You walk into the hall, and the stairs…there's a door leading to the hall…" Theo grew silent again.

"Yeah, you told me that. What else?"

"You know what? It's funny. I can't seem to remember anything about the place. Not even the exterior."

"That's not so strange. It was just a dream." Theo heard her words but did not believe them. He had had dreams before. They were scary, and they woke him up, but they did not return several times and, most of all, they never felt real. Theo could actually feel that he had been in the mansion walking around several times and he knew that there was something more to it.

The nights came and every time they did, Theo felt more and more scared of when the mansion would return. In a way, he hoped that it would just, so he could tell his wife exactly what it looked like. He would pay more attention to it and then he would tell her to prove that he was right, and she would have to admit that it was more than a dream.

It was in the middle of October, and nothing had happened for months. Theo had started sleeping properly again and, more or less, given up the thought of ever seeing the mansion again. Even though he still maintained it to be more than a dream, he could not but accept the fact that it might have been a foster of his imagination.

Theo went to bed and had no more than fallen asleep before he once again stood before the huge and unwelcoming mansion. Now he saw the exterior clearly.

Vines with sharp thorns climbed up the gray stone walls and the windows, despite their large size, revealed nothing inside.

The garden was bleak and almost indescribably empty of life. In spite of the fact that a number of plants grew there, they did not seem to have any color or even live. The whole place was more like a deserted graveyard. A place between life and death. Theo approached the massive oak doors leading into the mansion and, with all his might, he pulled them open and went inside.

Just as he set foot in the large hall, the doors behind him slammed shut and he was trapped inside. In a desperate attempt to flee, he threw himself against the large doors without any success. Theo fell to his knees in despair as he knew that he now was a prisoner inside his own mental mansion.

Theo twitched in agony throwing himself from one side of the bed to the other so violently that Carla was horribly awoken. The first sight she saw was her husband shaking spasmodically with his eyes rolled back into his head and blood dripping down from the corner of his mouth. She screamed to him, trying to wake him up, but he seemed to be in some kind of trance.

Quickly, she called an ambulance and they came and took him to a hospital. There was no response from Theo as he seemed to have gone into some kind of coma. He had stopped trying to bite off his tongue and was heavily sedated which kept him calm and relaxed.

Carla sat beside Theo and held his hand as the doctors ran every test possible to determine the cause but several hours later there seemed to be no answers and one of the doctors came in.

"Ms. Wilson, me and my colleagues have tried every possible thing, but we cannot find a medical explanation for your husband's condition. There is nothing physically wrong with him. It's almost as if…" the doctor went quiet for a second. "…As if he simply can't wake up." A chill went through Carla. She knew what her husband would say. His theory. But she did not want to believe that.

Theo woke up on the wooden floor. For some reason, he had passed out right after his attempt to escape. He looked around him. It was the hall of the mansion he had visited so many times. Why had he not remembered what it looked like? Now, as he was back, everything felt so familiar. The door to the dining room, the stairs leading to the balcony, and the bedrooms. He knew that he had been here before.

He went to a window to look outside. It was pitch black night. Theo shuddered. Night at this place meant more than nightmares. Knocks were coming from the second floor. Theo went closer. It was not knocking as much as it was tapping. Something tapping as it moved. As Theo came up the stairs, he could locate the sound. It came from the bedroom to the left. He went up to the door and gently touched the handle. No more had he touched it before a swarm of giant spiders crawled through the door making their way out into the mansion. Theo froze in terror but as they came closer, he ran for his life down the stairs and into the library and shut the door tight.

The spiders seemed to be caught in the lobby and Theo started looking for another way out. The library was large and had everything from books that looked ancient as time itself as well as obscure paintings of perverted fantasies. Theo recognized a few of the paintings for they were his own fantasies. Not the kind you talk about but the deepest and most twisted fantasies that you keep locked up deep within yourself. A horrible feeling went through him, but he continued searching for a way out.

At the very back of the library was a small wooden door that seemed to lead further into the mansion and Theo carefully pushed it open. He picked up an old-fashioned flashlight from a table and went in. It was an empty hallway. As he entered it, he noticed that it was full of statues. However, these were no ordinary statues for their bodies were twisted and their faces disfigured into horrid beings.

Theo got closer and as he shone the light upon them he could see that the statues were nothing but demonic versions of himself. Suddenly, the statues began moving and climbed down on the floor. Tormented screams echoed through the hall as they moved their twisted bodies closer to Theo as they chased him down the corridor.

Theo ran as fast as he could, trying to ignore the painful shrieks coming from behind him. Finally, there was a staircase leading up and in sheer panic, he ran up and through a door and closed it.

This whole thing was too much for him and now he was in the attic where there was no way to escape. The entire attic was completely empty except for a rope forming a noose hanging from the ceiling. Theo gazed at the rope in horror as he knew why it was there. He went up to it and looked at it long when he suddenly felt something.

A draft. Not much but still. He went up to the wall at the very end of the attic. It seemed fragile and as he examined it further, he noticed that the wallpaper was coming off and behind it was a hatch leading out.

Theo pushed it open and realized that he was right above the backyard. It was far down. Too far to jump without getting extremely hurt. He thought for a while and then he remembered the rope hanging from the ceiling. He took it down and used it to tie it to the hatch and started climbing down. It seems farther and farther to the ground and Theo made himself ready for another hellish surprise, but nothing happened and finally, he hit the ground.

Carla was getting impatient and felt that something needed to be done. Her husband had been asleep for almost two days and, still, no one offered anything that came even close to an explanation. She had been inside for far too long and though she did not want to leave him, Carla felt that she needed to get some fresh air.

The streets outside were dark and it must have been well after eight because the stores were closed, and most people had gone home for the evening. Carla kept walking until she came to a park. It was close to empty. Not even the dog owners were there and not a jogger was to be seen. For a moment, Carla felt uneasy as if this was a bad place to be but then she decided to have a short stroll down to the duck pond and then turn back.

She stopped by the pond and gazed out. So much had happened over the last two days and it was hard to get a grip.

"Don't be afraid," a voice said behind her. It was a little girl. "It's all going to be just fine."

"I'm sorry. What did you say?"

"It's going to be just fine. He just needs to find his way out." Carla was confused. The girl was way too young to be out alone this late and she seemed to have come from nowhere.

"How do you know?" Carla asked. The young girl giggled and ran off into the night. Carla did not have time to run after her but instead, she went back to the hospital at a quick pace.

Theo inspected the backyard. There were a few dead trees, and nothing seemed to grow beyond it either. The whole yard was surrounded by high fences with spikes on top making it impossible to escape. The only way to go was through the cellar door and back into the mansion. Theo felt an unease crawling through his body and the mere idea of having to go back inside scared the living hell out of him.

He pushed the cellar door open and came to a steep staircase. Left with no other option, he climbed the stairs and opened the door. As soon as he came up, he realized that this was a big mistake as he was back in the lobby and the spiders' nest.

By now, the entire lobby and hall were covered in thick cobweb and the spiders thrived in their new home. Theo did his best to lay low and tried not to catch their attention. The sound that the spiders made as they moved their jaws or spun their web was ghastly and Theo simply tried to reach the front door.

Somehow, he made it all the way to the door without being detected, and, as carefully as he could, he moved the handle and the door swung open. When Theo finally reached the stairs, there was another sound – a different sound. Something was flapping, like wings from something flying. Theo got a bad feeling and went back inside but the door was still open.

Before he could close the door, hundreds of crows stormed the mansion and the lobby only to get caught in the cobweb. The spiders came running and there was a short battle but most of the crows could not escape and were rolled into tight cocoons only to be eaten alive. There was a ghastly sound as the spider sunk their jaws into the flesh, crushing the bones of the poor crows slowly.

Theo hated both crows and spiders or feared them was more the right word, but this was far more than his mind could bear. With the spiders busy, he ran to the only door he could get to only find himself in the oddest room imaginable.

It was an ordinary wooden floor, but the room did not seem to have any walls, or at least they were too far away to be seen. The room seemed to go on forever and no matter where he walked there was simply no end to it.

Theo felt awful loneliness befalling him as if he would never be happy again. There was nowhere to go, and the door seemed to be miles away. He could not help but feel that everything was hopeless and there was no point in going on. Theo shed a single tear and then lay on the oak floor waiting for nothing.

The walk had done Carla good as she felt revitalized and strengthened in her belief. Even though she had no idea who that girl was, Carla felt that there was something special about her and as the door to the hospital opened, Carle walked in with a feeling that everything was going to be fine.

As she entered her husband's room, he was spasmodic once again and two nurses held him from falling off the bed while they waited for another nurse to bring more sedatives. Carla hurried in and held Theo's hand. All of a sudden, his body seemed to relax, and he went calm again.

"I'll sit with him," Carla said. "He won't need sedatives." The nurses agreed and left the room. "I'll be here, showing you the way out," Carla whispered in his ear as soon as they were alone.

Theo woke up abruptly not knowing exactly what was going on. He was not sure if he had slept or if he passed out but, no matter the reason, he was still in the endless room but this time something felt different. A presence he could not explain. He got up on his feet and looked around. There was a small door, no larger than a cabinet but still a door and possible way out of this god-forsaken place. Theo lunged himself toward the door and came out into what appeared to be a kitchen.

There was a cooking pot and skinned animals hung from meat hooks in the ceiling. In fact, everything in the kitchen seemed to be dead animals. There were chopped-up rabbits, beheaded pigs, and ripped open deers with their intestines hanging from their bellies.

Being a lifetime vegetarian, Theo felt sick to his stomach by the horrid sight and just barely did not vomit. Suddenly, all the dead animals woke up simultaneously and screamed in terror and before Theo the until just now, fresh meat rotted, and large, white maggots ate their way out through the skin of the poor animals as their screams faded away.

The floor was covered with maggots and Theo ran through the only door available only to find himself in a dead-end. It was nothing more than a storage room with supplies. He looked around for something to use and stumbled on what appeared to be a hatch. Whether it had been there a moment ago, Theo could not tell but he was running out of options, and whatever horrors were before him was better than to go back.

Theo fell down the hatch and simply could not stop falling until suddenly he fell into water. He struggled to reach the surface and as he finally could breathe again, he realized that he was in a lake in some sort of cave. The whole lake was surrounded by steep, razor-sharp rocks and it was more than ten meters up to the hatch. In all, it was more of a well of which there was no escape.

An almost black sort of mist shaped itself on the surface and took the form of a robed figure. Slowly, it came closer and closer. Theo panicked and swam as fast as he could away from the figure.

Everything had gone just fine for so long but now Theo's vitals were getting worse and worse by the minute and he was twitching horribly just like the first night. His muscles were cramping as he held a tight grip around Carla's hand and would not let go. Whatever belief she had mustered up began to fade away once again.

The nurses held Theo and awaited a doctor who would come and assist them in controlling the situation. The doctor came running and they got ready to give Theo enough sedatives to put him to sleep for at least a day. Carla felt horrible despair and looked out through the window for a sign and just across the street on the sidewalk was the little girl from the park again. She seemed to stare right at Carla with a most resolute look. Carla understood and just barely stopped the doctor from giving the shot.

"Wait! Wait, just one more minute," she told them.

Theo swam around in circles trying to avoid the black-robed figure following him in a most unnerving way. All of a sudden, something grabbed hold of Theo's leg and pulled him down underwater. Theo struggled but whatever had a grip on him was way too strong and he got pulled beneath the surface. From below he could see the robed figure aimlessly searching for him with no result. Theo felt that he was running out of air and very slowly it went dark. From there everything went very fast as he was lunged out of the mansion and back into his conscious mind and abruptly, he sat up straight in the hospital bed throwing up masses of water.

Drowned and Buried

"How is this even possible?" Green asked befuddled. "I just came from a pouring London hoping to see some sun and I arrive at a rainy desert. Would someone be so kind as to explain this to me?" He was an elderly man who felt that he was too old for jokes.

"I'm just as shocked as you are," a voice behind him said. It was his associate Dr. Amira Quasim. She was difficult to see under the thick coat she was wearing to shield herself from the weather. "It started just a day after we began our excavation. This is highly unusual."

"Indeed," Green added. The workers made their way through deep areas of mud and around them, the sand kept collapsing making it nearly impossible to get any kind of work done. Green looked around him. This was a futile endeavor. "Call it off for the day. Let's hope for dryer weather tomorrow." Amira nodded and made a quick gesture with her hand to signal that they should stop and both herself and Green hurried inside a tent.

Once inside she got rid of her coat which was soaking wet and heavy as a result. Amira reached for a towel and began to dry her hair. It was dark and had a silk-like texture to it that Green had always admired. As for himself, he was bald and sadly not by choice. To tell the truth, it had been a long time since he could do anything with his hair on purpose. On the other hand, he had a nice goatee to make up for the loss.

Amira was finished drying herself and offered him a towel. Green who was also finished drying himself using nothing but a napkin politely declined her offer.

"Talk to me, Doctor. How is this possible? It's raining more here than in London, for God's sake!" Green said despairingly.

"We don't know. The weather was perfect a few days ago but, on the night, after we started the excavation, the rain came. The forecast said nothing about it and they still don't. It's as if the rain is localized directly above us."

"Don't be absurd! There is no such thing!"

"Then why don't you stick your head out the tent and explain this to me because I can't." In spite of Green's very recent arrival, Amira was beginning to feel upset. She was a highly renowned archaeologist with a doctorate in Egyptology and not a weather woman on Channel 5 and she did not feel like arguing about a weather phenomenon.

"I'm sorry. This whole mess has me worried to death. Not only will it slow down our progress and diminish our chances of finding anything at all, but there is also a great risk that the rain will destroy many of the artifacts in the crypt."

Suddenly, they were both interrupted by intense singing and chanting outside. Green peeked his head out. An old man wearing nothing, but robes lay on top of a muddy hill and prayed on his knees.

"Is he a worker?" Green asked.

"No, that man has been following us ever since we left Cairo. He believes that we will bring down the wrath of the ancient gods upon the land."

"Really? And why does he think that?"

"Well, according to legend, this is a holy temple of Osiris, god of water and death and he believes that we have disturbed his sacred slumber." Amira waved her arms around theatrically and, suddenly, she chuckled. "You can imagine the look on his face when the rain started pouring down."

"Yes, I'm sure it was a very horrifying experience for him." Green seemed lost in mind as he stared into the distance.

"Oh please! Don't tell me that you believe this guy? I'm a religious person too but this is nothing but the delusions of a mad man. He has done nothing but disturbing the workers and chanting nonsense. My only concern is that he will scare them away."

"I see. Well, he is clearly mad as you say," Green said, lighting a cigarette. He did not care much for cigarettes as he found the taste to be far too bland. The only time he actually smoked them was when he was traveling. The pipe was far too fine to risk but at the same time, he could not stand to be without nicotine for long. He smoked half the cigarette and then disposed of the rest.

Amira coughed, more as a silent protest than as a real reaction. She had known Green for many years and considered him to be a good friend but she had never gotten used to his smoking. He had many fine qualities such as good manners and a fine taste for art and culture so it was a shame that he had to smoke. Not that she was interested in him, she just thought it was sad that he ruined his health and above all, she hated the smell of nicotine.

Green seemed far too preoccupied with other thoughts to notice her protest and, for a moment, Amira wondered if he even noticed her presence.

"Harold?" Amira asked. Green quickly turned around with a face most surprised as the only one who used his first name was his mother. Amira tried not to care. "What are you thinking about?"

"Oh, it's nothing. Nothing at all. Everything just seems so strange."

"Hey! I told you not to get all superstitious now. We have to focus on the excavation. Everyone is working as hard as they can to get as many of the artifacts to safety as possible. When the rain stops, we have to work fast to save whatever is left to save. The workers cannot wade in deep mud."

"No, of course not. Excuse me, Amira, but I'm really tired after my trip so I think I'll retire for the evening."

"So soon? I was hoping we could use the time to identify and categorize some of the findings but sure. Whatever you want."

"I know, I know, but I'm far too tired to be of any use to you anyway." Green saw that she was disappointed, but he felt exhausted and the whole situation had him puzzled.

Once in bed, he listened to the dripping sound of water falling down on the roof. It was a steady stream and it seemed to increase rather than clear up. Green tried not to let his imagination carry him away, however, he could not but think that this was strange. Of course, Green had seen heavy amounts of rain before. He lived in London after all but there it was a completely natural thing and something you just had to deal with. Here it was a hot summer in the middle of the desert, and it was wet like a humid London day in November.

Morning came and the first thing that Green noticed was the all too familiar sound of raindrops hitting the roof creating a cacophony of sounds. He could tell just by the sound that the rain had increased. He got dressed and took a look outside. There was a thick and odd morning mist surrounding the entire place making it difficult to see anything at all. Being British, he could instinctively tell that whatever this weather was, it was not about to stop anytime soon. Suddenly, he saw Amira running around trying to wake everybody up. Green hurried outside.

"What has happened?"

"The roads we built down to the excavation site…" Amira started, and you could see the stress in her eyes, "they are gone." Green put his coat on and followed Amira out to see what the commotion was all about. He could instantly feel that the sand had become wetter. The rain and the mist were hard on it. Apparently, one of the workers had tried taking a car out of here and the road had given in. It took no closer inspection to realize that it was only a matter of time before the entire hillside would erode.

"This was the only road here," Amira said with a deep sigh.

"So, we're stuck here?"

"I don't know," Amira answered. "I simply do not know."

Everyone had stopped digging for the moment and instead they worked on possible ways to leave the excavation site. One idea was to build ladders leading out of the rain but no matter how they tried the mud made it impossible to build anything that could hold for long.

"We will have to call for aid," Amira said. "I will attempt to send a message to Cairo about our situation. Until help arrives, the only thing we can do is to keep excavating the tomb."

The workers did as she said but Green could see growing disbelief in their eyes as if they knew that help would not come. The rain kept pouring down and with more and more intensity. The fog seemed to grow thicker by the minute making it impossible to see anything and Green stopped to think for a moment. There was something wrong. Something missing, and he suddenly realized that he had not seen the sun once since he got here. He went to Amira's tent to tell her about the observation only to find her deeply upset.

"This is serious," Amira said, pacing back and forth.

"What's wrong?" Green asked.

"I've tried to reach someone in Cairo, but I can't get a signal with any of our equipment. It's as if we are inside a magnetic field or something because all of our transmitters are stone dead."

"But surely someone must be looking for us?" Green said.

"I doubt it. We're far out in the desert and unless this storm spreads no one will know that we are in danger."

"What about food?"

"We have some supplies, but they will not last long. I would say that we have food for a few days, maybe less."

Green felt a shiver running through his entire body, and he had a strange feeling that he was being watched. He turned around and saw someone quickly disappearing from the tent entrance. Green hurried to see who it was but no one was to be seen.

"Damn!" Amira said. "Now the whole excavation will know the gravity of the situation."

"But we would have had to tell them anyway," Green pointed out.

"Yes, but now they will think that we've tried keeping the truth from them. We might have a riot on our hands."

They went outside to get a feeling of how many knew of the situation. No one spoke to them. Everyone they met just stared at them in silence, but Green could see that the disbelief he saw earlier in their eyes had turned to an ominous mix of anger and hatred and to make matters worse it rained more than ever. The raindrops now hit the ground like tiny missiles and even for an experienced Londoner, this was a lot.

"You have to say something to them," Green whispered to Amira.

"I know," Amira answered with a trembling voice. She got up on a crate and tried to speak up as best as she could. "My friends, what you probably have heard is true.

No help will come for us and we are running low on food. I'm not going to lie to you. It looks bad. If we don't receive any help, I fear we have only a few days left and then we will sleep with the mummies. So far, our tents can handle the rain but it is only a matter of time before they give in."

"What about the tomb?" someone in the crowd said.

"What about it?" Amira asked.

"It's made from solid rock. We'll be safer in there than out here." A group of workers applauded him.

"That would not be safe, I'm afraid," Green added. "The tomb is at the very bottom of the valley. When the valley gets flooded, and it will, I'm afraid, the tomb will be the first thing to go."

"So, what do you suggest, Doctor?" the man asked. Green turned silent. He did not have a suggestion and he feared telling them the truth, which was that if someone did not help them, they were doomed.

After the meeting, which was more of a decree of slow and sure death, Green felt worse than ever. This was his excavation and he was the founder and the reason why they were all here and now he was responsible for these poor souls who would most likely never see daylight again.

That night, Green went to bed with a heavy heart. As he lay in his bed, he was struck with a sudden fear that this might be their final night and he stayed awake listening to every single drop of rain that came crashing down upon the roof assuring them a watery grave.

Morning came and Green felt quite relieved that it actually did. It was still pouring outside and the water level had risen so much that the entire floor was flooded. He put on clothes and boots and waded up to one of his backpacks where he pulled out something wrapped in a blanket and then he went out.

The hillsides were crumbling and huge chunks of sand were moving almost like avalanches down on the outer regions of the excavation. The workers had started piling crates in hope of shielding themselves from disaster. It worked for the moment but it was obvious that it would not withstand the force that would be unleashed when the entire hillside would crash down upon them, and that was inevitable.

Green observed the workers as they put their heart and soul into what they were doing, and he felt more and more guilty. He went to see Amira who was busy trying to save artifacts from being destroyed by water. He went to her desk and slammed the seemingly heavy package on it.

"What's that?" Amira asked and her voice held no patience.

"That," said Green, "is the reason why we are here. Go ahead. Open it." Amira went to the desk and started to carefully unwrap the blanket. Inside it was a stone tablet with ancient hieroglyphs.

"What does it say?" Amira asked. Green sighed and sat down in one of the chairs and stared at the tablet as if it was unholy or cursed. Words did not seem to come easy to him and Amira tried her best not to be insensitive but, at the same time, she was stressed about the whole situation.

Green pulled himself together and explained, "I acquired this tablet on one of my journeys. It was buried in a tomb in Tunis and I brought it to London for closer inspection. The hieroglyphs talk of a place with great fortune and riches. I interpreted the symbols and got a location. This place."

"And?" said Amira who felt that there was something more to the story.

"And there is something else. The tablet speaks of a warning. It's hard to translate exactly but at the bottom of the tablet it roughly says, 'Death to those who attempt to claim the treasure'."

"So, you think that just because an ancient relic tells you to stay away, this is all your fault?"

"Don't you? The warning is quite clear."

"No, Harold. No, I think not. I think that you are being paranoid, and that you need to stop blaming yourself. This storm has nothing to do with ancient warnings I tell you—" Green was about to say something but was interrupted.

"Not another word. There is no such thing as curses or evil gods. Now, do not speak a word about this, do you hear? I've got an entire camp of scared workers who are so terrified that they are ready to believe just about anything and the last thing I need is complete panic. Is that clear?" Green did not know what to say. He thought that Amira would be mad at him but not this way and now he felt like a rambling mad man who believed in superstitious nonsense but at the same time he had no explanation for the weather phenomenon.

"Listen to me now," Amira said to him, and her voice was much calmer now. "Do not tell anyone about the tablet. That would be a disaster. I will store it here in my tent and keep it hidden. Remember, this is not your fault." Green knew that she meant well but no matter how much she tried to calm him, Green could not help but feel guilty. He left the tent and decided to help the poor souls who were working hard at building a wall of crates around the tents.

"What was she so upset about?" a worker asked. Green nearly asked the man how he could know that Amira had been upset but remembered that the walls of the tent were thin. He stopped to think for a moment. Was this a test? How much did this man know? After a brief consideration, he decided to say nothing.

"She is just stressed," Green said, hoping that the man would accept the answer. The worker said something he could not quite make out and went back to work and Green hoped that there would be no further questions. He was still uncomfortable having to lie to those he had basically killed.

After a day that seemed like it would never end, they had finally managed to build a wall that would keep the sand and the water away from the tents for a little while. Green's back was aching and he had serious problems just sitting in a chair. He was not in his prime any more, that much was for sure but at least he felt that he had done something to help. He decided to go to bed early and hope for a tomorrow.

Sleep eluded Green but, finally, he passed out from feeling worn and beaten, when he was suddenly awakened by the roaring sound of thunder. Green got to his feet quickly and ran out of the tent wearing nothing but a coat and boots only to find that the rain had turned into a proper thunderstorm. The workers were up too and they had taken what they could carry and were heading down to the tomb.

"What are you doing?" Green yelled at them.

"We're saving our lives!" a man answered him. We have a much better chance of survival inside the tomb than we have out here."

"But don't you see it will get flooded?"

"Perhaps, but if we stay in our tents during a thunderstorm, we'll be toasted." Green did not know what to say. The man had a point but before Green could talk him out of it, the man was gone. Green ran to Amira's tent and she was desperately trying to get hold of anybody using the equipment but there was no use. Green ran up to her.

"We have to escape! The whole place is about to collapse on us!" Just as they exited the tent, there was a tremendous roar and the lightning struck the hillside causing the tomb to be buried under heavy masses of wet sand.

"Climb! Climb!" Green yelled to Amira who started climbing on one of the remaining hillsides. Green was right behind her and for a second, he actually believed that they would make it. Then the sand started moving downhill. With his last breath, Green stretched out his hand to give Amira an extra push before everything caved in.

The desert had returned to its original state and there was not a single trace that there had ever been an excavation and the sun was shining bright in the dry desert. Suddenly, Amira's hand reached up through the sand and someone dragged her out. Although her eyes were covered with sand, she could see who it was. It was the mad man who had been following them from Cairo.

"I told you not to anger the gods but you wouldn't listen."

Happy Birthday

Aaron slowly began to recover his eyesight but everything around him was still one big blur and, on top of that, his head hurt badly. The air around him was thick and humid making it hard to breathe and a stench of ammonia hit his nostrils like sharp razors. Aaron tried to get a feeling as to where he was, but he was far too dizzy to even begin to comprehend the gravity of the situation.

The last thing he could recall was taking a late evening stroll around the block when everything suddenly went black. The culprit must have come from behind because he could not remember a single thing except for the blow to the back of his head. Aaron gently caressed his head feeling a large bump that was extremely sore.

He tried to focus, tried getting a grip of his whereabouts. Slowly, very slowly the world around him became clearer, and he could finally see where he was. It was dark and the walls were made from solid concrete. Apparently, he was trapped inside some sort of silo. A faint light came from the very top of it. A window perhaps or just a bright lamp. Way up in the middle of the silo was a huge claw-like crane hanging in wires.

There was no reasonable explanation as to why he was here. Abducted, yes, but there was no sign of a culprit. Suddenly, there was a moan as in pain coming from the other end of the silo and it was not until then that Aaron thought to have a look around him. He stood a good while just staring at the surroundings wishing he had not for the entire bottom of the silo was covered with passed-out people. Men, women, young people, old people, all there for some reason.

The moans from the other end of the silo increased and Aaron made his way over there without accidentally stepping on anyone. The cries came from a young girl no older than fifteen. She too had regained consciousness and stared at the obscurity while trying to process what she just witnessed. She looked at the people and the crane, and then at Aaron.

"You... you..." she began. I could see what she was implying and began waving my hands frantic in objection.

"No, no, I did not do this! It wasn't me! Look here, I have a bump in the head too. We were both abducted. Taken away against our will, see?" Aaron turned and showed her his wound. She seemed calmer, not calm by any means but at least for now, she did not suspect him.

"What the hell is going on here?" she asked.

"I don't know, I simply do not know," Aaron responded. "I woke up just minutes ago to find all this. Do you remember anything as to how you got here?"

The young woman shook her head. "All I can remember was jogging in the woods when I took a sudden blow to the head and then I woke up here."

More people began waking up, all telling the same story about doing something ordinary outside and then being abducted. No one seemed to have seen the culprit. It was as if a ghost had attacked them out of the blue and brought them here.

All of a sudden, bright lights came on and from old rusty speakers, the "Happy birthday" song echoed out in the entire silo while colorful balloons and confetti came down from the ceiling. The whole thing was bizarre and most wicked. As they stood in complete silence as the birthday decorations rained down upon them, a voice was heard from the speakers.

"Hello, can you hear me? Is this on? Hello, my friends, and welcome to my birthday party. Over the night you and I are going to have lots of fun! I bet you are all wondering what you have done to be the lucky chosen one to be invited to my party? Well, you see there is one thing that I have wished for most of all and that is a new friend to play with and that is why you are all here. You all could potentially be my new BFF. Oh my God, we could have so much fun together, you and me. Tormenting people, slaughtering stuff, and creating some lovely mayhem. But let's not get ahead of ourselves. I still don't know who it will be, do I?"

An elderly lady with a cane looked straight up the silo and screamed out, "You're sick! Do you hear me? Sick! You need a mental institution, not a friend!" Suddenly, the crane started moving at a fast pace. The woman tried to escape it, but the crane swooped down and caught her by the waist and lifted her way up in the air.

"That's a boring and negative attitude," the voice said whereon the crane opened dropping the lady all the way down to the concrete floor. Parts of her flew all over the place and the young girl next to Aaron shrieked in horror.

"I hope we can all get along from now on," the voice said. "Now, behave, soon there will be cake." The bright lights were turned off and everything went back to being pitch black.

Although everyone was awake, there was a strange silence in the air. No one said anything, no one moved. People just sat on the concrete floor staring into the dark like frightened rabbits trying to escape the butcher. Some of them seemed to find a way to come to terms that this silo would be their final resting place while others still tried to process the image of the old lady breaking against the floor.

"Come on, everyone!" Aaron tried. "We're not doomed yet! Let's not give in to this maniac. We can get away from here if we only work together!" Not a single person said a thing. He might as well have been alone in the silo. He looked over at the young girl and, for a quick second, their eyes met.

"Do you believe it?" she asked.

"Yes, I do! I have to believe it! We can survive this if we stay together."

"That's a nice way of looking at it," a person behind Aaron said. He was tall and had a big beard. "A lovely speech there. The name's Peter by the way."

"Aaron."

"I'm Kayla," the young girl said, and only then did Aaron realized that he had been too shocked to ask for her name.

"All right. That's pleasantries, now how are we going to get out of here?" asked Peter.

"I don't know," Aaron responded. "Let's think about this for a moment. We were all brought here meaning that there has to be a door of some sort somewhere in this silo."

"So simply check the wall?" Peter answered.

"Yeah, I mean we've all been so busy trying to grasp the situation that we have not checked for a way out."

"True. You and Kayla go that way and I'll go this way. There has to be a door or a hatch or something," Peter said. They started walking with their hands stretched out in front of them. The bright lights that came on earlier had really blinded them making it almost impossible to see just about anything further away than their arms could reach.

Suddenly, Kayla yelled, "Hey, guys! I think I've found something. It's a hatch! Get over here and help me push it open."

"Where are you?" Peter's voice echoed through the silo.

"Over here! Follow my voice." After a good while, both Aaron and Peter had found their way to Kayla. It was a hatch indeed. They all tried pulling it open, but it seemed to be shut tight as if it was barred from the other side.

"Damn!" Aaron said. "Whoever is doing this to us sure has it all planned out." The lights came on once again making it almost impossible to see. Aaron peered, trying to get a glimpse of the interior. It was big, huge even and most of the people were rubbing their eyes from the light.

"Well, this is the saddest birthday party ever!" It was the voice from the speakers again. "It's like you're not even trying to have any fun. Come on now. Let's turn those frowns upside down! Who wants cake?"

"Sure, get in here and blow the candles so I can break your little neck!" a man said.

"Is that any way to talk to someone on their birthday? So rude! Didn't your mother teach you any manners? Never mind, I'll teach you." The crane started moving again and at a furious speed, it followed the man across the floor. This man however was younger and far more agile than the old lady so he managed to grab hold of the crane and climb on top of it.

"Hey! That's cheating! No fair!" the voice said and you could hear the annoyance in the voice now.

"Yeah, what are you going to do about it?" the man taunted the speakers. Aaron was a simple man who did not claim to know much but he did know that teasing your kidnapper was a bad idea no matter how you looked at it. All of a sudden, the crane started swinging furiously from one side to the other but the man hung on.

"You are one persistent little bastard, aren't you? It's almost a shame to kill you."

"Well, you're not doing a very good job with that either, are you now?" A single shot echoed loudly in the silo and the man fell dead to the floor.

"I said almost a shame, didn't I? I hate guns. They are so primitive but he gave me no choice. Anyway, don't let this spoil your appetite. Have some cake." From a small hatch, a birthday cake was pushed in whereon the hatch was closed again.

"Nobody touches it!" an elderly woman said. "It's probably filled with cyanide or something."

"Right," Kayla said.

"Well, what are you waiting for? Eat it!" the voice said.

"It's poisonous," the elderly woman said.

"No, it's not!" the voice responded, sounding quite offended. "Think about it. I want a new BFF. How can I get that if you're all dead?"

"Oh, screw it!" a younger man said, as he ran up to the cake and took a large bite of it. "Look, I'm eating it! Let's be friends forever, you and me. Here is your new BFF!" Only seconds later froth began forming around his mouth and he lay on the floor twitching spasmodically in pain.

"Don't you know that it is the birthday child who gets to cut the cake?" the voice said. "Where are your manners?"

"I said it was poisonous!" the elderly woman yelled. "You swore it wasn't!"

"Well, no one would have died if you only had followed the rules of a birthday. This is your fault really."

Aaron looked at his watch. They had been here for about two hours and already three people had been killed and there were eleven people left in the room. This was going too fast and he began realizing that before anyone would find them, they would all be dead.

"Anyway, I'm going to turn the lights off for a while but stay tuned for more fun to come. Who knows? I might even have a present for you guys even though it's not your birthday. Aren't you excited? I know I am. This is the best birthday ever! See you soon." The lights went out and everything went back to being dark.

"Everyone, come closer to me," Aaron said, trying not to be too loud. "Let's try to think about this. We know that whoever is up there can both see and hear us, right? So there have to be cameras and microphones around the place. We should try to find them. Make that maniac blind or deaf."

"I agree," the elderly woman from before said. "I actually saw one of the cameras. It's on the crane."

"Great!" Aaron said. "What about microphones? Has anyone seen any?"

"You know that guy who climbed the crane? What he said? He did not say that very loud and still the kidnapper heard him," Kayla said.

"What are you trying to say?" Aaron asked.

"Have anyone checked their clothes?" Suddenly, the lights came back on, and the voice echoed from the speakers once more.

"Okay, we're having so much fun! Fun, fun, fun! Who wants presents?" the voice said most stressed.

"The microphones must be in our clothes," the elderly woman said. "Find them!"

"No! Do not remove any clothes. I will let you all go free if you kill that old hag for me. She is ruining the fun!" Everyone began undressing down to their very underwear.

"I found one!" Peter said. "It was hidden in my jacket. Throw away everything." They threw all clothes in a pile far from where they were and now they all stood in the middle of the silo, like a frightened herd waiting to be hunted by a predator.

"No, no, no! This is all wrong! You're doing it all wrong! None of you are good enough to be my best friend. I'm going to pick you up one by one and shake you until you realize what's good for you." The crane came down once again like a huge arm and although everyone tried to dodge, they all stumbled over each other. Peter was big and easy to catch. Just like that, he flew right into the air screaming in pain. The crane shook him like a stuffed animal, threw him against the wall and he fell bleeding to the ground.

"Peter!" Aaron yelled coming to his assistance but he was nothing more than a sack of flesh and broken bones. "I will get you, you hear me? You monster! You freak!" Aaron screamed.

Kayla came running. "Shut it or you'll get us all killed!"

"I'll kill that maniac!" Aaron cried.

"Will you please be quiet? Breathe." Aaron did his best trying to calm himself down. Everything felt futile as if they were never going to see daylight again. The few remaining persons were in the hand of someone who clearly had no intentions of leaving any survivors. The speakers came on again.

"Okay, I know that we haven't really gotten along and I'm ready to admit it's all your fault, but I also want you to know that I'm willing to forgive you. Give you a second chance because that's just the kind of person I am. A warm and forgiving person. So, let us all start fresh. I'm even going to give you all a present even though it's you who should be giving me. Isn't that nice of me?" From the ceiling came colorful presents down strapped to balloons.

"Do not open them!" the elderly lady said in a strict tone. "It's a trap!"

"Why aren't you opening them? I bought gifts for everyone. Not opening them would be rude and we all know what happens to rude people, don't we? Now open them!" A few of the victims picked up a present.

"It's the only chance we've got," a middle-aged man said looking at the present as if it was infested. They took off the ribbons. Kayla, Aaron, and the elderly lady backed away as if they knew something bad was about to happen. The others carefully opened their presents.

"What is it?" Aaron asked.

The middle-aged man stared down in the box as if he had seen his deepest nightmare come to life. His voice trembled as he stuttered a few words: "Spiders... The whole bloody box is full of big spiders!" He threw the present on the floor and hundreds of angry spiders escaped the box.

"Mine is full of giant centipedes!" another one screamed.

"Rats! Big fuckin' rats!" someone else yelled and in the blink of an eye the entire floor was filled with rats, spiders, and centipedes. It was like the most horrid scenario imaginable. People shrieked in terror as they attempted to climb the concrete walls all in vain.

"Look, I got you little pets to play with? Aren't they cute? And, look, we're having so much more fun now! You should be thanking me. Why aren't you thanking me? Ungrateful bastards!"

There was an awful sound as the hungry rats ran across the floor searching for food. The elderly lady who had stayed with them was far too slow and Aaron witnessed as a horde of spiders made their way up the poor woman's body. The screams and the noises that she made as the venomous arachnids injected their nerve toxin in her cut through Aaron like sharp knives. The lady fell to her knees becoming easy prey to the starving vermin who stormed her, feasting upon her tender flesh until the wounds and the venom from the spiders got the best of her. She cried out for help but was silenced as a rat ate its way down her throat.

This was more than Aaron's mind could handle and, in a final attempt of survival, he pushed Kayla toward the rats but, somehow, she managed to make a quick move causing Aaron to slip and fall. The spiders swarmed all over his body and Aaron could do nothing but wait to be devoured and left in shreds. A final thought of disappointment came over him as he actually somewhere believed that he would make it.

There was no one left alive now but Kayla. She felt betrayed by Aaron in spite of the fact that they had only known each other for a few hours. He had seemed like a decent person but it did not matter now. Nothing mattered any more for she could not do anything but wait to be eaten alive. She lay on the cold floor crying with no hope whatsoever when suddenly the voice from the speakers came back on.

"Get up! Stand up!" it said in a most demanding voice. Kayla did her best to rise and saw as the crane picked her up into the air. It had a tight grip on her, and it hurt a lot but at least she was safe from the spiders and the rats for now.

"We're finally here!" the voice said. "The moment we've all been waiting for. You are the last one alive so I now present you with a choice. You can either choose to fall to a dreadful and most certain end. By now, you know that there is no escape and if I drop you, you will be crushed and eaten alive…" The voice paused for effect. "Or I can save you. Pick you to be my new best friend forever and we can do horrible and unspeakable things to the world until hell brings us home." Kayla stared into the pit that could be her final resting place, and, in a sudden desire to live, she screamed with all her might:

"Please let me live! I'll do anything for you! I promise to be the best friend you have ever had!"

The voice giggled. "That's what I wanted to hear." The crane went far up toward the very top of the silo and there it dropped off Kayla into a small hatch in the wall. Kayla was blinded by tears and the bright light and the only thing she could hear was a voice saying, "Welcome, Kayla! My very own BFF!"

My Lady in the Painting

I lay in my bed pondering the events of late gazing upon the cracks in the tile ceiling. It has been several weeks since the passing of my late wife Elena but sleep still eludes me. I have tried many things in order to find comfort in my existence but I cannot accept her destiny, and I am still tormented by a grave feeling that has been growing inside of me. It is not out of some sudden notion of self-pity that I have come to this conclusion, it is merely a fact. It should have been me.

Everything started during that dreadful autumn when all was gray and the rain kept pouring down for several weeks. Having been cursed with a lack of patience, I grew increasingly irritated and could often be found wandering the corridors of the house up and down in the restless pace of a person who has not seen the sun for far too long.

My wife and I bought the house six months ago after having lived in a small apartment in town. It was sheer luck really that we found the house. Apparently, the husband who lived in the house before us committed suicide and his wife died shortly after that from what was explained as grief. Soon after that, the house was put up for auction, and I and Elena bought it.

The house was a dream come true as we both had long wished to find a place in the countryside away from all the stress and the noise of the city. Being an architect, I am in need of peace and quiet to be able to work and the school where Elena works is closer to where we live now so we bought it without any further consideration.

The real estate broker told us that the house was very old and apparently built sometime in the nineteenth century. The information about who built it and who lived here first had been long lost or perhaps forgotten and therefore the broker could tell us very little about the origin of the house. I keep writing "house" when manor is probably a more appropriate description for the place seemed huge for only me and Elena but bear in mind that we planned to extend our family as soon as we had finished fixing the place up. This was before everything literally went to hell.

The events which ultimately led to the deterioration of us both started, as I mentioned earlier at the beginning of the most dreadful autumn anyone had seen in many years. The rain kept pouring and pouring down turning everything to a muddy field making the smaller roads especially the unpaved ones lethal to drive any kind of vehicle on resulting in many days indoors with no sunlight.

I am not trying to say that I need sunlight, but I tend to get very easily annoyed when I am denied fresh air. The first days went fine, and I managed to keep myself from becoming a total nuisance to my environment but after a while, a restlessness began to grow within me. I started working on small projects around the manor just to keep myself occupied or perhaps going crazy, I do not know. My wife found my projects to be quite disturbing as I would lose myself completely in whatever I was doing and when I became like that time and days mattered very little to me.

I could stay awake for several days and I would only be seen when my hunger became so intense that I physically needed to eat in order to stay alive. I lost a lot of weight and from time to time I could feel my body getting weak although I did not tell Elena as I did not want to alarm her. I convinced myself it was for her sake, her own good, but it was really for me since I was terrified she would call a doctor and have me hospitalized.

When I had finished a project, I would wander the premises like a restless shadow or a ghost just waiting for the next idea. I wasn't going anywhere, I barely left our garden. I just went around looking for a project to fall into my hands.

One day, I decided that I would take on the task of drawing every room and make a collage of paintings in a private gallery. I do not know how it came that I made the discovery that I made. Perhaps it was sheer luck or maybe someone wanted me to find it but I soon discovered that there was one room missing. It was clearly visible from the outside since the walls on the left side of the manor were far too thick for the room inside. I was thrilled like a child that had found a buried treasure and I decided to find out more about the room.

I got a yardstick and started doing measurements in order to determine the size of the room and I realized that the room had to be very small. Tiny in fact. There seemed to be no windows in the room for the concrete was old and untouched. I became obsessively determined to locate the door which led inside. During this time, I barely ate, I spoke very seldom, and my sleep was limited to when my body simply could not stay awake any more. Sometimes, my dear wife would find me almost literally climbing the wall trying to find some sort of secret passage.

One day, when she came back from her morning walk, she was completely stunned for I had torn down every piece of wallpaper in the rooms adjacent to the room. My fingers were covered in deep red blood and my nails had been scraped off to the very bone. In spite of all this, I cannot remember myself being in any pain. I was hardly aware of the gravity of the situation. This caused my wife to call an ambulance. I fought back at their attempts to tend to my wounds so I was given a shot and when I woke up, I found myself in a hospital bed with my hands tightly wrapped in bandages. I could tell from the number of bandages that had been used that it was far worse than I could have possibly imagined.

For several days, I was hospitalized and they forced me to see a shrink, a psychologist. I had to talk about my recent behavior and I assured everyone at the hospital that I was feeling much better and I really did. I do not know if it was the fact that they forced me to eat or if I just needed a change of scenery, but when the day came for me to go home, I felt refreshed and full of energy. I apologized to my wife and promised her that I would make it up to her as best as I could.

For once I felt full of life and I could not wait to get home and start the life that I and Elena so often spoke of.

That feeling was withheld up until I set foot in the hallway. I could feel it immediately. All the feelings. The obsession, the need, the room. It was an awful feeling and I tried to shake it off as soon as I felt it, but it was too late. The seed had been planted and for the next following days, my mind was preoccupied with finding the room.

I did not say anything to Elena, of course. Had she suspected anything I would have found myself back in the hospital in no time. Instead, I started doing research in complete secrecy. I hid notes and started searching every single possible place where one might hide a hidden door. At first, I found nothing and I began to consider tearing the very wall down but I was afraid to damage the contents of the room so I restrained myself and kept on looking.

It was not until one day when I was actually not looking that I made progress in my search. My wife had made the suggestion that I should try and read something in order to get my mind on more healthy things. I followed her advice and I got really caught up in the book. I still wandered the hallways but at least I was occupied with something else and one day I was walking down a hallway that I rarely walked when I suddenly hit my foot on something hard under the carpet. I could not see what it was but as I lifted it to look, I found it to be a metal handle attached to a hatch.

Immediately, I felt a curiosity swelling up inside of me like a rising tide and I let myself get controlled by the same urges that had put me in the hospital. I removed the carpet and found a heavy-looking hatch. I pulled it wide open only to find a ladder leading into a dark basement I had never seen before. My wife was not around to stop me so I let myself get carried away and I grabbed a flashlight and went down into the dark.

When I came down, I realized it was not so much a basement as it was a corridor. A tiny and very narrow corridor. I could tell that no one had been there for a long time because the air was damp and I had to clear the way from thick cobwebs. I admit I felt a growing sense of unease as if something wicked awaited me at the end but my urge and my need to know overcame my fears and I ventured on.

At the end of the corridor, there was a rusty iron ladder leading up to another hatch and without any greater consideration, I opened the hatch and went up. As soon as I entered the room, I felt a great sensation of accomplishment and I realized that I had found my secret room. It was everything I had hoped it would be. White sheets covered old Victorian furniture and the bookshelves were filled with old dusty books. Instantly, I could feel that the room had been untouched by the decay of time because I could see that every single piece of furniture was perfectly preserved.

On the wall, just in front of me, there was a gigantic painting carefully wrapped in more sheets and I felt an aching desire to unwrap it to see what was behind. As I started to take down the sheets one by one, I had the weirdest feeling as if this was something I should not be doing. It was a feeling of something old and very evil but compelled by my uncontrollable instincts I kept on removing the sheets until the painting was fully revealed.

I took a few steps in order to be able to see the painting in all its glory. It was a woman, seductive and alluring and I felt myself being captivated by her beauty. The complexion of her skin was so lifelike that I almost could touch it. Her cheeks had been painted to look as if they were soft as silk and I swear I could see every single straw of hair. And then there were her eyes. Those tempting dark eyes seemed to gaze right into mine, filling me with a warm and comforting feeling. As I stood there mesmerized, I could almost feel her neat little hands caressing my body.

I sat down in a chair and for hours I did not do anything but stare into her perfection. Since the room had no windows, I quickly lost track of time and when I finally decided to return to my wife, I didn't even know if it was day or night. The only reason I took my eyes from her was that my stomach literally was aching badly. I went back down the hatch and promised myself that I would return as soon as possible.

II

When I came back up, I could hear the distinct sound of muffled voices coming from the hall. I went to see what all the commotion was all about and found my wife with two police officers. When Elena saw me, she basically threw herself in my arms and started crying while muttering the phrase, "where have you been, where have you been?" over and over again.

Unaware of the situation, I asked what was wrong and one of the policemen informed me that my wife had reported me missing. My spontaneous reaction was anger and I asked her why she could not let me be along for just a few hours.

"A few hours?" she replied, sobbing. "You have been gone for three days."

At first, I refused to believe what she told me and, instead, I accused her of being delirious but the two policemen confirmed that what she said was true. I excused myself and went to the big hall mirror my wife had insisted on buying and stood staring at my reflection. It was clear that I had, in fact, been inside the room for three days without noticing it; my beard had grown wild and my cheeks looked thin and sort of dehydrated because of the lack of nutrition. The police offered to take me to a hospital for further examination, but I kindly passed on the offer and assured them that I would be fine.

After they had left, we sat down to eat. It was obvious to me that Elena was mad at me, but I pretended like I could not see it and instead I focused on eating. All my thoughts were on the mysterious lady in the painting and I could not wait to see her again.

The dinner table was filled with various dishes and it seemed like every bit of food we owned was on the table. My wife had some bread and wine and nibbled the edge of the bread in a most disliking fashion and I could tell this was not a good time for conversation. I did not mind and instead, I went directly for the grilled chicken which I devoured almost whole leaving nothing but bones. I know

I should have been full after such a meal but no matter how much I stuffed in, I still wanted more. After finishing the chicken and one pork chop, I felt thirsty and I poured several glasses of wine. Normally, that would have been more than enough to make me a bit tipsy but today it felt like I might as well have been drinking water. No matter what I ate or drank I just could not feel the satisfaction of having eaten for my mind wandered back to the room and the lady.

Later that evening, I was filled with a great urge to go back and I almost did but I knew that if I disappeared again so soon, my wife would surely put me in a hospital or, even worse, an asylum. Instead, I helped myself to an extra-large whiskey and tried to find out more about the lady. I searched every book in the house and tried to find old articles, but nothing came up. It was as if she had never existed.

That night my dreams were uneasy and I saw the room go down in a lake of fire and death. From the fire, I could hear a woman's voice screaming out to me, "Why, Wesley, why?" I woke up screaming and every single muscle in my body was tensed and I was sweating uncontrollably. Elena was awakened by my screams and wondered what was wrong but I ordered her to go back to sleep.

Long I lay pondering the dream and, suddenly, I heard the same voice as the one in my dream echoing through the dark halls of the manor. I got out of bed and tried to find out where the voice came from. She whispered something. Words, but too low to make out. Too curious for my own good, I kept looking and, suddenly, her soft voice became clearer. She was whispering my name. *"Wesley, Wesley."* There was definitely sexual tension in the way she said my name and I found myself being drawn down into the hatch. I followed her voice back into the room again. It was her. I should have known it from the moment I heard her voice for only a beauty like her could have such a tender voice. I sat myself down in a chair and did nothing but admire the perfection before me.

Days seemed to pass but I felt no pain nor agony as I sat in the chair bewitched. The bones in my body began to feel like dry wood and my fingers like old sticks ready to crack. I quickly lost my strength and even moving from the chair started to feel like an impossibility. Somewhere deep inside of me, I think I knew that people were looking for me, my wife above all. It had been some time since I gave her the slightest thought and for a brief moment, I wondered how she was doing.

However, I tried not to think about the outside world too much. My lady in the painting did not like it when I thought about other women. It was her and me now. Every day she would caress my body and soul with her gentle hands and raise me to a state where I felt almost godlike while whispering words of love in my ears.

Suddenly, one day, I heard the distinct sound of footsteps coming our way. I guess they must have found the hatch after an immense search. My wife, Elena, was with them as they carried me out of the room. I wanted to resist but by now my body was so weak I could not stand and barely speak. Two men in white coats helped me down to the entrance and when we came down, I saw myself in the mirror.

To be honest, I did not recognize my reflection. My beard had grown completely wild and my skin was hard like dried meat. My once so attractive hazelnut-colored hair had turned pale white like that of an old man. I tried to shed a tear but even my very tear canals seemed to have been dried out.

To my left, I glanced at my wife. Her face on the other hand was full of tears and she looked as if she had had a thousand difficult years. Her grieving for me had left her old and wrinkled around her eyes. I felt myself being struck by a sudden feeling of shame and disgust over what I had done to her, but I was too dehydrated to even attempt to contact her, and before I knew it, I was hooked up to tubes and taken away in an ambulance.

For several days, I did nothing but sleep and could not dream of anything but her. My lady. She still whispered to me. Small words of affection but there was also a disappointment in her voice I had never heard before and she wondered where I had gone to. When I explained to her that I was in a hospital because my wife was worried, her affection and concern turn to blind rage and jealousy against my wife, and she swore to avenge me. I tried to implore her not to hurt my wife, but she was gone. I woke up with a horrible headache but alive. A nurse came in to check up on me. As I could speak again, I took the opportunity to ask her how long I had been gone.

"A month," she answered shortly. To say that her answer stunned me is a huge understatement and I sat perplexed pondering what she had said. "You do know that everyone has been looking for you like crazy?" she continued. I shook my head as I still struggled with grasping what had happened. The nurse gave me a strong sedative and I fell asleep.

Once again, I dreamed of my beautiful lady in the painting but this time she cried out my name in pain and there were flames and death. Suddenly, there was another cry. A voice I knew all too well. It was the voice of my dear wife. I woke up screaming in pain as if someone had burned me alive. The nurse came in running and asked me what was wrong. Terrified, I grabbed her scrubs tight and yelled in her face, "Fire! So much fire!"

"Sir! You need to wake up! You are dreaming!" I know that she was trying to calm me down, but I instinctively knew that something was wrong. Another nurse came in and gave me a sedative to make me more relaxed, but I knew. The witch in the painting was up to something.

The next day I received a letter from my wife saying:

My dear Wesley,
I can only hope that a few days of rest will do you good and I look forward to your return. However, I am afraid. Afraid of the room, afraid of the painting, and afraid of what will become of you if you return and the painting is still here. To tell the truth, it terrifies me. Therefore, I have made a decision for you. I will burn everything in the room and then I will have it smashed to the ground. I am doing this for you, for us.
Your dearest wife,
Elena

Knowing the lady would never allow herself to be so easily disposed of, I threw myself out of the bed in sheer desperation in a futile attempt to save Elena, but my legs were still too weak to carry me. The second after two policemen showed up. They told me that there had been a horrible fire in my home and that my wife had passed away in it. Unable to fully grasp what I had just been told, I became mute. The policemen told me that everything we ever owned had turned into ashes except for a single painting which was inexplicably unharmed.

Play with Me

The garden lay before him like an endless wasteland and not the slightest shade was to be found. Withered leaves and wilted flowers covered the ground and not even the birds seemed to enter their land. The new house was like taken from a ghost story and completely secluded from the rest of the neighborhood. It was not even the last house on the street, but they had to continue on to a small path a few hundred meters into the forest after the last house to come to theirs. Obviously, he had protested when the news of the move came since all of his friends were far away now.

The new school could also be good and perhaps he would find new friends here too but right now, it was nothing he was the least interested in finding out. Right now, the move here was a punishment and the new house a prison that he could not escape. Gently, he took a few steps out of the prison yard and looked around. It was surrounded by dense deciduous forest, although no leaves appeared on the trees any longer.

His mother had gotten a new job in the middle of the coldest November and they had been forced to move at once. The punishment was in grade to be deported from their homeland and put behind enemy lines just to be abandoned and left behind. There was a slight breeze through the forest and the trees whistled a tune that sent shivers down his spine. It was as if they called to him in the same way as you would attract a dog.

Henry was only nine years old and had been endowed with the natural curiosity that all boys at that age have, but now he wanted nothing more than to run back to his parents and try to forget that the forest was there. He turned and walked back toward the house, but with every step, he took the music seemed to rise like a furious crescendo until it was way too high for just being an unusually melodic whistling in the trees.

He was now standing on the top of the doorstep and was about to open the door and enter when he suddenly heard someone laugh behind him. As from an instinct or a reflex, he turned around quickly and began breathing heavily. "I did not mean to frighten you," said a bright boy voice. Before him stood a little boy no older than himself, dressed in a vintage school uniform-like attire. The little boy pondered Henry who still struggled to regain composure. "What is your name? Want to play?" the boy continued.

"Henry," Henry replied, and he noticed that his voice was trembling. It was absolutely not okay if you were about to start first grade so he calmed himself quickly and responded with a significantly steadier voice that he certainly wanted to play. The little boy opposite him laughed again and ran into the forest. Henry ran after without thinking anything about it. He was surprised how deep the wood stretched and it became increasingly difficult to determine from which direction he had come from.

Eventually, they came to a glade among the trees, and Henry thought he could glimpse a playground a little further up ahead. The moment he approached the playground, he felt a strange feeling coming over him. It was as if all his anguish over the move was gone and all that he had previously whined about was blown away for in front of him appeared the most amazing playground anyone could have ever imagined. Swings and climbing frames were surrounded by an entire field of beautiful flowers. The flowers smelled of a thousand different wonderful scents and for every breath he took, he felt a little more carefree. Henry stood paralyzed with wonder and could do nothing but stare at the beauty around him.

"Are you okay?" the boy asked who saw that Henry had stopped behind him. Henry made an effort to get a grip and nodded. He was just about to ask how the little boy could have found this place when the boy suddenly ran toward one of the climbing frames and swung himself up. "You cannot catch me!" he shouted, and Henry felt a euphoria go through the entire body and he ran after him.

It had been dark for long when Henry finally got home. By that time, his parents had been thoroughly worried and he had to go straight to bed without food as punishment. All night he dreamed of the beautiful field with flowers and the amazing playground. Henry came from a relatively large city, where there were several large playgrounds but not one came even close to this one. The next morning, he woke up to someone outside throwing pebbles at the window. He hastened to open and saw that it was the little boy again. Quickly he ran down, had a sandwich, and hurried out.

"Will you play with me?" asked the boy in the same remarkable way as the day before. Henry reacted to the almost unnecessary, and a bit contrived, question but said yes since he still wanted to play; it was a sunny day for a change, and the two boys ran away through the woods to the playground where they played until Henry had to go home. The little boy ran in another direction, and Henry ran through the woods and arrived at the house.

It was not until then he discovered that he had had so much fun that he completely forgot the jacket at the playground. Without thinking more about it, he ran back through the woods just like the boy had shown him but no playground was to be found. The forest was thick around him and neither flowers nor trees seemed to thrive. The whole thing was like a barren wasteland of intrusive shrubbery and decaying leaves.

Suddenly, it started to clear up and he came out into a small clearing in the forest. The playground was gone and the only thing there was a wooden cross like the one you use to mark a grave. The cross had once been white with a metallic plate in the middle but was now rotten and half destroyed. Henry went up to the cross and began cleaning the plate from moss. It had the name "John" on it. No surname or date of birth or anything, just "John". Henry felt a sudden chill go through his entire body, and for a while, it was like the very blood in his veins turned stone cold. He looked around him and found his jacket hanging in a tree not far from the grave and he grabbed it and ran back home as if his very life depended on it.

When Henry closed upon the house, he could feel a scent of homemade cooking spreading through the air and he hurried inside and slammed the door tight shut. Once indoor, he just stood in the hallway for several minutes gasping for breath. All the way home through the forest he had a dreadful feeling that something or someone was following him. No, chasing him like prey.In the kitchen, his parents sat by the dining table and waited for him.

"What is the matter?" his mother asked. Henry thought that he ought to tell them about the boy and the playground and the grave but for some reason all he could say was, "Nothing, I was just really hungry."

"I see that you found your jacket. That is good," his father remarked. Henry made an effort to calm himself down and sat on one of the chairs and ate. Although the food tasted delicious, Henry could not bring himself to enjoy the meal. He was still too shaken up and the food seemed to be growing inside his mouth and had a slight aftertaste of putrefaction. "What is the matter?" his mother asked in a most displeased tone. He then realized that she must have seen his contempt for the food as he made an effort to smile. "Nothing. It is delicious!" he said and added the thumbs-up just to be safe. His mother seemed a bit happier, and he choked down the rest of the meal which now tasted only of ash and rotten flesh.

His father forced him to wait by the table until everyone had finished and directly after that, Henry announced that he was tired and wanted to go to bed. Even though it was a most strange thing for Henry to say, his parents bought it and he was excused. Once in the bathroom, he filled the toothbrush with as much toothpaste as the brush could hold and then he put some extra in his mouth and then he started cleaning it out as best as possible. He brushed every single corner but no matter how he tried, he just simply could not rid himself of the foul taste. Finally, he gave up and went to bed.

That night, he did not sleep. He just lay in his bed, staring into the white ceiling in hope that the little boy would be gone forever. The events of late were far too much for him and the taste of rotten corpse lingered in his mouth like a culinary nightmare. Of course, he had never tried corpse apart from the meat his mother cooked but that was different. That was fresh. This was rotten and strange and... and... evil.

Dawn came like an unwanted visitor and peeked inside Henry's bedroom window. He never had a problem with mornings before, but this particular morning he did not want to get out of bed. Although the daylight kept pouring in the room, he pulled the bedspread further up his head until it covered his head completely. For a long moment, he just stayed there, afraid to move or even breathe, carefully listening for any sound outside. There were not any. No sound of footsteps on the driveway and no pebbles gently hitting the window. He was not there. No one was there. The only sound was Henry's mother making breakfast in the kitchen as usual.

Henry had a slight feeling of hunger and decided to defy his fear and get out of bed and walk down the staircase. The boy was not there. Henry felt a wave of relief go through his body. It was not until then that Henry realized that yesterday's events really had gotten to him. The moment he relaxed his muscles, he became exhausted and felt a need to catch his breath. He sat by the table with a plain slice of white bread, not even roasted and his mother looked at him as if he was sick, but Henry did not even notice that. He was busy trying to conjure up enough courage to taste the bread. He was afraid. The foul smell had all but vanished and he did not wish to taste it once more. For a very long moment, he just sat there, looking down upon the piece of bread as if it was his greatest enemy but finally he decided to have a bite. His jaws clenched together and processed the food in his mouth. It tasted bread. Simple, white bread. And quite boring without any butter on it. Henry took another deep breath of relief and finished the breakfast. He even ate more than usual.

After the meal, he decided to try his luck even further by going outside. It was cloudy but still a warm day. He gazed upon the jacket he had retrieved yesterday but decided to leave it at home. For some reason, it still gave him chills. Once outside, he realized that a shirt was more than enough for the air was moist and warm just like after rain on a hot summer day. It was a bit strange, however, that it was this hot at this time of year but he did not think about it any more and went outside to play. Henry felt like a cat discovering snow for the very first time as he took one tiny step at a time away from the house but not so far that he could not run back inside if he wanted to. After a while, he had gotten to the point where he was quite certain that he was alone in the garden. He had gone to the outer parts of the yard where the forest begun and stood in complete silence and glared out into the wicked shrubbery.

Suddenly, he got a feeling that someone was watching him from somewhere. It was quiet and not even birds seemed to be singing but, still, it felt like someone or something was breathing right next to him. Henry turned around and found himself face to face with the boy.

"You will play with me," the boy said. His voice was darker now. More grown-up and far more demanding. Henry got ready to run back to the house, but the boy looked at him with an evil smile. "Do not even think about running. This is a maze. You will be running until you drop dead." The boy chuckled and pushed Henry in front of him. Suddenly, the boy's voice changed again. "Why did you have to go back? That grave was not for your eyes."

Henry looked back at the boy. "John, is that your name?"

The boy stopped abruptly and seemed to zone out for a while. "I do not remember. I do not think that anyone does." Henry turned around and could see in John's face a fear, deep and very honest.

"Was it your tombstone that I saw?" Henry asked, dreading the answer. The boy still glaring out into the distant nodded in silence and now he looked as if he was about to shed a tear. "I feel sorry for you…" Henry said trying to sound as well-meaning as he possibly could. The child broke down in tears and covered his face in the palm of his hands. "It is going to be all right," Henry tried. In the very instant as he had said those words, the boy's cries changed into a burst of terrible laughter and as he looked up, he had a grin upon his face so evil that it sent an ice-cold shiver down Henry's spine.

"You pitiful human being! What makes you think that you know anything about me? What gives you the right to judge me? I know your kind. It was your kind that left me to rot in this godforsaken forest!"

"I'm truly sorry about what happened to you! I really am!"

"Of course, you are. All the other boys were too. Shedding their pathetic tears for me without meaning any of it."

"I mean it! I swear!"

"Silence!" The boy's voice was dark and had the sound of an adult. "Keep walking!" Henry turned and kept moving forward, too afraid to speak. "We are here," John said. Up until now, Henry had not considered where they were going but he immediately recognized the place. They were back at the dreaming playground but this time everything was different for no beautiful flowers bloomed and the wonderful scent was gone. Instead, everything around them seemed to have withered and there was a foul smell of decay in the air that Henry recognized all too well. It was the smell from yesterday and he covered his nose in pure instinct. The boy chuckled once more and pointed at the now rusty merry-go-round shaped like little bicycles. "Sit!" he said demanding and as Henry sat upon it, the boy started to speed it up. At first, just a little bit but then faster and faster until Henry had to hold on as hard as he possibly could. Henry looked at the boy and begged him to stop but the boy just grinned even more and continued to give the merry-go-round an almost demonic speed. Henry looked at John with a pleading look which only seemed to give the boy further joy. All of a sudden, through the furious speed, Henry could see John's true face. It was a putrefied face heavily eaten by worms and worn down by the many years of decomposition. Suddenly, the boy burst into mad laughter so bad that his jaw cracked and from the broken jaw and the molten teeth, Henry could hear the words, *"Play with me!"*

Pest

"I still have to say that the whole place creeps me out."

"Don't worry, Jessica. It's old, not evil." Mike gave his girlfriend a look of amusement. "Besides, it was really cheap so the money we didn't spend on buying the house we can now use to refurbish the place. It'll be great."

"Yeah, I know, but I still think we could have stayed in the apartment until the house was finished."

"And keep paying that ass of a landlord his expensive rent? Honey, you know we can't afford that. The guy was ripping us off and, besides, I like it out here in the countryside. The air is fresh and we actually have a garden. Do you know what the first thing I am going to do tomorrow is? I am going to pour myself a hot cup of coffee and sit on a chair in our garden and listen to the birds singing."

"Oh my God. Just because we have a house doesn't mean that you have to get all poetic all of a sudden."

"That is a great idea. Maybe I should. I'll start writing weird poetry and wear berets all the time."

"Go ahead. And I can move to a place in town and get a sane boyfriend," Jessica said, taunting Mike. Mike laughed and ran inside the house.

"Come on, slowpoke!"

The next morning, Mike was up early full of enthusiasm to get started on the house. Jessica, on the other hand, had the look of someone who had not slept for over a week. She made her way to the coffee maker and poured herself an extra-large cup of pitch-black coffee. Mike was ready to give her a comment but hindered himself as she glared at him with burning eyes that clearly said not to utter a single word until the cup was empty.

Mike also sat with a cup but he only managed to take small sips since the coffee was scalding hot and he was afraid to hurt his tongue. This, however, did not seem to bother Jessica because she was gulping it down as if she was drinking ice coffee.

"Honey, is something wrong?" Mike tried asking her carefully. Jessica raised her hand in a gesture to wait a moment whereon she emptied her cup and refilled it.

"Rats."

"What?"

"Rats, Mike. Do you know those little bastards with claws and tails? They pretty much caused the whole plague disaster in the medieval ages. You ever heard about them, Mike?"

"Of course, I have," Mike answered, knowing that there was no right answer to her question.

"Oh good. That's really good, Mike. And do you also know that this house is full of them? Yeah, that's right. They're in the walls running around at night."

"Are you sure? It might be anything." Mike heard himself just after he had said the sentence.

"I sure hope you are not suggesting that the sounds coming from the walls is something worse 'cause in that case I say we burn this place to the ground and build an entirely new house." Jessica gave Mike a look that told him she was clearly not joking, and he hurried to change the subject.

"Hey, you. Let's just calm ourselves down by getting rid of all the junk in the shed outside and you'll feel better once it's a bit cleaner." The shed was just across the house and had been built to store wood but the only thing in there now was tons and tons of old things left by the previous owner.

"No, not yet," Jessica said. "First, we clean the house. I know it will not do much but if we are going to stay here, I want this place to be spotless. When that's done, we can start clearing out the shed." Mike who was set on starting to fix the shed sighed but then again, the house was truly filthy so they might as well start there, he thought.

Jessica started fixing up the bedroom and Mike got started on the kitchen. The cabinets in the kitchen were full of old canisters of dry products such as flour, baking powder, and oat. There were enough ingredients to bake a cake. He opened the can labeled flour but was startled as it was swarming with meal beetles that apparently had their own little society in there. He went out and emptied the entire can in a shrubbery and went back inside.

Just as he went up the stairs, he was thrown out of balance by a horrid shriek coming from Jessica in the bedroom. Mike ran as fast as he could up the stairs to get to her but was nearly pushed down the stairs again by a hysterical Jessica who tried her best to get down and away from the bedroom.

"What is it? Please tell me what the matter is," Mike tried.

"What the matter is? What the matter is? Do you really want to know what the matter is? Well, then, Mike Yeats, I shall tell you what is. Have a look in that opened cabinet." She was pointing at a cabinet opposite of the bed and Mike slowly went inside to take a closer look. He had to admit that the sight made him sick to his stomach for in the cabinet was the corpse of a giant rat. It was obvious that it had been there for quite some time because the skin had melted, and maggots ate their way through the leftovers.

"That's the matter," Jessica said angrily. "You make sure to get pest control here right away. I don't care what it costs. I don't care if we have to work triple shifts to afford it. Hell, I don't even care if you have to sell one of your kidneys to afford it. Do I make myself clear?"

Mike, still shocked from the sight, wasn't paying attention to her yelling and simply nodded in reply.

That night they both slept in the car and the next morning the pest control was there to cleanse the house.

"Do you want us to do the shed also while we're here?" the pest control asked. "I should tell you that it will cost extra."

"No, just do the house," Jessica answered. "That's enough."

Some hours later, the pest control was done. "Okay, it's clear to go inside again but I agree. That was bad. If I were you, I'd get rid of all the old furniture and get new because it's in such a bad state. Anyway, you take care now. I left a few cans of bug spray if you need it." The car left the driveway, and they were alone again.

Mike ran up to the door, put his arms out, and yelled in a goofy euphoria, "This house is clean!" Then he ran in while dancing a weird kind of dance. Jessica gazed at him and sighed but she had to admit that she was genuinely relieved that she could enter the house without having to be scared.

The night was surprisingly comfortable and the next morning not even Jessica could find anything to complain about. Of course, there was a lot to be done before she would consider calling it home but having a pest-free home was a good and most necessary start. She even looked forward to a nice day out in the garden fixing it up. The sun was bright and she saw this as an opportunity to get some tan.

Mike put on gloves and got ready to clean out the shed while Jessica armed herself with garden tools and went for the flowerbeds. Mike stood in front of the run-down shed. The paint was all but gone and the hinges on the door were so rusty that the door almost fell off. There was no point in keeping the shed once it was empty and Mike planned on tearing it to the ground and then building a new one.

It was a risky move as Mike knew very little about any kind of construction. He and his brother had built a treehouse when they were young but that was about it and the treehouse had crashed to the ground just a week or so after it was done. Luckily, no one was hurt but their mother had forbidden them for making a second house.

However, Mike believed in learning by trying so he was determined to build the new shed himself even if it would take months. Before he could do anything, he needed to empty the old one out and now he was staring angrily at a huge pile of rubbish. First of all, he began dragging an old bike out. It had rusted completely and wheels were stuck in a fixed position. After a closer inspection, Mike threw the bike on the ground and decided that it had to go.

Just after he had thrown the bike, he felt something tickling his arm as if that something tried to move upwards and in an instinctive reaction, Mike tried shaking it off. It turned out to be a small spider of some sort, not frightening by appearance but quick on its feet. Mike shook it to the ground and it disappeared.

He then reached into the shed to find more things to throw away but was startled to find what appeared to see that the entire shed was full of these little bastards. As it would seem, they had made their nest there because further in thick cobwebs covered every little piece of rubbish.

"Jessica!"

"What now? What did you find? Not a dead corpse, oh please, don't let it be a dead corpse."

"What? No. And by the way, a corpse is dead, to begin with, just for your information."

"Who made you a grammar expert? Seriously, what have you found? Keep in mind that I just barely got through the last surprise."

"Yeah, yeah, whatever. Check this out." Mike lifted an old box in the shed in a single corner and a dozen spiders ran out.

"Mike, what the hell! So, you will fix the shed by yourself. I'm not getting remotely close to that spider-infested pile of garbage, you hear me?" Mike chuckled, and Jessica went back to the flowerbeds muttering words like "filthy" and "disgusting". Mike went in to get a pair of gloves and then he continued to empty the place while doing his best to ignore the spiders.

It was in the middle of July, and the weather was scourging hot and after just an hour or so, Mike was sweating like a pig and huge drops poured down from his forehead and into his blue eyes causing them to itch. Mike raised his hand to try and clear the sweat but as he was rubbing his eyes, he felt a slight tingling in the corner of his left eye as if something quickly crawled behind the eyeball and disappeared within him. Mike threw off his gloves and began jumping around while screaming in sheer horror. Jessica came running as fast as she could.

"What happened? Are you hurt? Should I call an ambulance?"

"A spider! A goddamned spider crawled in behind my eye!" Jessica stared at him long as if she was processing what she heard but then she burst out into laughter.

"Are you laughing?" Mike was furious.

"Seriously, Mike, am I supposed to believe this? You're just trying to freak me out, but it is not working so quit it."

"Jessica, for crying out loud! I'm not joking! There is a bloody spider behind my eyeball!" Mike's voice got more and more high-pitched.

"Oh, stop it! Do you know, Mike? You're not as funny as you think you are. I'm going to have a beer in the sun. You can join me if you promise to stop this paranoia act."

"You think I'm being paranoid?"

"Paranoid or cruel, your choice. Now, how about that beer?"

"No, I'm good. I'm going in to lie down a bit."

"You do that, but beware of the tiny killer spiders." Jessica giggled and sat down in a chair. Mike chose to pretend not to hear. He was busy with his thoughts. Was there a spider in his head or was he simply being paranoid? He did not know. Tired from recent events he lay on the temporary mattress, gazing up in a crack of the ceiling. Slowly, he began dozing off as if he was going to fall asleep. Mike stared at the crack. It was quite large, and Mike wondered what had done it. All of a sudden, a leg of something big came through. It was not a human leg for it was black and had a crablike form. Mike's entire body grew stiff as he was too afraid to even move a muscle. Just as the ceiling was about to break open, Mike
woke up screaming.

He did not know how long he had slept but it was significantly darker outside. He was beginning to get a mild headache and his eyes itched as if they were dry. On top of that, his hearing had become somewhat muffled and a bit wobbly. He wandered down to the kitchen to get a painkiller. Mike did not check what time it was but it was most definitely late. Jessica had had one too many beers and was sleeping in the chair on the patio.

"Hey, sleepyhead!" Mike called out to her.

"Look who's talking, sleeping beauty. I can tell that you have been sleeping too." Jessica turned around. "Oh my God! Are you all right? You look terrible and I mean really terrible."

"Thanks for the kind words but no, I'm not fine. I think I might be coming down with the flu or something."

"Oh no! Not now when we have so much to unpack!"

"Gee, some sympathy…"

"Oh, I'm sorry! You poor thing! Feel better?"

"Whatever. I'm going back to bed." Just as Mike went back up the stairs, he felt an itch in his nose and a sudden urge to sneeze. There was no paper around, so he sneezed in his hand. As he pulled his hand away from his nose, he noticed that it was covered with thin web-like strings. He shuddered and found himself doing nothing but stare at it in a desperate attempt to comprehend what was happening.

Perhaps Mike was unable to understand the gravity of the situation, or perhaps he chose not to understand it, but, with a simple gesture, he wiped it off on his pants and decided to go back to bed. It was probably like Jessica said. He was being paranoid about cleaning out the shed and on top of that, he was sick. Some more sleep would definitely clear his mind and get him back on track quickly.

Hours passed and it was way over midnight but Mike still could not find any peace. There was persistent pain in him that kept growing and in the back of his mind, a sharp tone grew louder and louder. It annoyed him. Made him angry. Mad. No sleep in the world could cure whatever ailed him. He went back down.

Jessica was obviously drunk for she slept on the patio although slept was a far too nice word. Passed out or hammered seemed to be a far more accurate description of her state. She did not even wake up though Mike stumbled around in the kitchen in a desperate hunt for painkillers. At first, he thought they were all gone, and he was ready to take a sledgehammer to his head just to make the pain go away but then in a drawer, he found a couple. He filled a glass of water and swallowed them down and even swallowing came hard to him.

It was three in the morning, and he was determined to get some sleep before sunrise so he went back upstairs and lay on the bed. Mike's entire body hurt as if he had been exposed to third degree burn wounds. He got up and ran into the bathroom and ripped his shirt off. The mirror could not lie but he still had trouble comprehending what he saw for his entire torso was filled with rash, like nothing he had never seen before and on top of that he had blisters that seemed to be filled with something that looked like white puss.

He scratched a blister and it immediately burst and a liquid poured out over his chest. Quickly, he wiped it off and while doing so he could swear that he saw something moving underneath his skin. Mike backed away from the mirror as if it was an evil entity and sat on the side of the bed. There he sat until dawn. The few moments when he was able to fall asleep from sheer exhaustion, his dreams were filled with morbid visions of himself drowning in an ocean of spiders making their way inside of him and then eating their way out again.

Awoken by panic, he forced himself out of the bedroom and down the stairs to the kitchen where Jessica made coffee. She turned around and looked at him. For a moment, she was about to say something but then she remained mute.

"Honey? Is that you? What has happened to you?"

"What are you talking about?" Mike responded annoyed.

"Don't freak out now but you have some kind of reaction. Your eyes are swollen and you're pale as a vampire. I'm calling an ambulance." As she lifted her phone to make the call, she was interrupted.

"Honey?" Jessica said.

"Yeah?"

"There is a spider crawling out your ear."

"Are you kidding me?"

"No, and now there is one coming out your nose."

"Honey?" Mike said shortly.

"Yes?"

"It hurts." Mike began twitching and, suddenly, every blister on his body exploded as a thousand spiders burst out at once. His screams echoed as the spiders ate him from the inside making their way over to Jessica. Jessica grabbed two cans of bug spray left by pest control and began spraying as she ran for her life out to the car and drove away.

The Horrible Secret of George Wagner

It all began on a gray day when the desire to be outdoors did not turn up as it usually does. I have always found that there is something relaxing about nature that has always appealed to me and I took my hunting license as soon as I was big enough to follow my father into the woods and hunt game. Ever since then I have not missed a single opportunity to hunt, and I cannot even begin to describe the calming effect it has on me to sit quietly far out in the woods just watching the surroundings. To be completely honest, it doesn't even matter if I get to shoot something, it is the feeling of being out in nature that soothes my senses.

It was in the middle of a hunt that I met George Wagner. A reclusive gentleman who had just retired and was now enjoying his long-term vacancy so to speak. He was nice and seemed to have a healthy outlook on life. He had a taste for fine whiskey and on the road, we started talking. I happened to have a bottle with me which I kindly shared with him during one of the evenings in the hunting lodge. We discussed topics such as politics, philosophy of life, and general hobbies whereupon we discovered that we had more in common than one might think.

The more the evening turned into night and the bottle began to peter out, we drifted into the subject of love, and I told him that my wife had left me many years ago and that I now lived alone. He expressed regret and said that he also lived alone since his three former wives sadly left the earth life too early. When the last wife died, he simply had not been able to start again and now he lived with his two hunting dogs alone in a house. I expressed my condolences, and he must have seen that I was a bit troubled because, suddenly, he changed the subject abruptly and began to talk about his greatest hobby.

As it turned out, George's biggest passion in life in recent years was taxidermy, better known as the art of stuffing animals. He had stuffed a number of animals that he had hunted but he also helped others who came by with well-preserved carcasses. At times, he also aided various museums or other clients who wanted different animals, and thus he had made a name for himself in the business.

We decided to hunt together for the rest of the week and I must admit that it was one of the nicest weeks I had had in a very long time. Once the week was over, we parted with the promise that we would keep in touch, and he even promised to stuff an animal for me for free as a thank you for the whiskey I had shared with him. We thanked each other for nice company and went back to our respective homes.

Call it coincidence or whatever but just a few weeks later I shot a fox that had such incredible fur that it was absolutely fantastic. The colors were amazing and it was soft as velvet and I instinctively thought that it would be magnificent as stuffed so I called my friend and asked if his offer was still in force. The question was almost rhetorical as he was overjoyed to hear my voice.

Said and done, I packed my stuff and headed down to him the very same day with the animal and looked forward to once again get to philosophize about life's vagaries with my newfound acquaintance. However, I must admit that I was utterly astonished to see that his house was very secluded. It was a long way into the small, hilly forest roads that barely existed on the map before I found my way. It was really sheer luck that I decided to take the jeep that day for the road that led up to the house left a lot to be desired and I had gotten stuck with my other car.

Finally, I closed upon the house, which was surrounded by pines and birches which, curiously, seemed to be leaning away from the house as if they were uncomfortable having to stand so close to it. It was a natural phenomenon I had never seen before despite my many years as a hunter. The farm was simple and left much to be desired. Sure, I have never been a man who claims that a garden is needed, but here there was almost no lawn to speak of as it was more green moss that had spread everywhere. A pair of rusted cars stood half shoved in the woods and there were piles of what I would call junk in each and every corner.

When I went into the yard, I was met by George who shook my hand and wished me welcome. He also apologized about the road and assured me that he had been meaning to do something about it. I replied that there was no harm done and we entered the house. The interior was just like the rest of the farm, very simple. A few paintings hung on the walls and the wallpaper was obviously old as it was timeworn. The only room that was well decorated was the living room which to my big surprise was cozy and inviting. The walls were covered with bookshelves full of old books and a hefty cabinet was placed on one of the sides with plenty of whiskey and other spirits. There was even a fireplace which I could tell from the fresh ashes was working. Furthermore, there were several of his stuffed works in different parts of the room, including a full bear which was stuffed in a standing position. I stood amazed and admired the magnificent animal.

"I'm very proud of that," George commented as he held out a beer for me. He snuck up on me so quietly that I jumped in pure reaction. He apologized and we started to talk about the art of stuffing animals. "It's not just doing it, you know. The basic idea is pretty simple but it's getting them to look alive that's the trick." I could see that he had a special glow in his eyes when he talked about such things. It was clear that he did not often have visitors.

George asked me to sit down, while he was preparing the animal I had brought with me for preservation. I sat down in one of the armchairs that looked very comfortable and waited for him to come back. Once he got up from the basement, he asked if I would like to stay for dinner. I was in no rush and I really wanted to talk to him some more so I decided to stay.

Time went by and we ate and drank well until it was late and my friend asked if I wanted to stay. Of course, I said "yes" and he prepared one of the guest rooms for me.

Long into the night, we sat and talked just as we did in the hunting lodge and I was happy that I had found a kindred spirit. Eventually, the effects of one too many drinks become obvious and we decided to retire for the night.

I guess it's pretty common, but spirits have always had a strange effect on my bladder because I need to visit the toilet every five minutes. Getting there sober in a new house was hard enough but to get there in the condition I was in turned out to be easier said than done. After having fumbled around in the dark while trying not to wake George, I finally found a handle that I supposed led to the bathroom and I turned it and the door opened. I started looking for the button to the light and soon concluded that it was a chain from the ceiling. I pulled the chain and the light came on abruptly.

The sight was so horrid that I instinctively felt dizzy, and I had to rub my eyes to be sure that my mind was not playing tricks on me. Inside, I was greeted by a sight so morbid and disgusting that even the most callous person would be shocked. Whatever created this was not human or in the total absence of any human emotions. Before me were three young women stuffed and dressed in beautiful gowns with jewelry. All of them looked surprisingly calm. Their skin was smooth and there was something odd about their faces that gave them a sad expression. Their eyes were clear in color and really lifelike but still there was a dead feeling to them as they stared into nothingness as the ghosts of those they once were.

"It's strange," I heard behind me. "No matter how hard I try, they always look sad. You cannot really get them to smile. But now, at least age will not hurt them any more." I had not noticed that George had woken up and was now standing just behind me. "They are beautiful, are they not? I hope you if anyone can appreciate a masterpiece when you see it. The trick is not to harm the body. I use lethal injection. Minimal damage and they feel nothing."

Horrified, I pushed my former friend aside and ran terrified through the house and out to the car. For some reason that I still do not know, he did not follow me but remained in a window contemplating my escape. When the car started, I gassed violently out on the road because like the forest I wanted to get as far away from the house as I possibly could.

Here Lies Walter Smith

I can hear them. Their tiny feet clickety-clacking against the roof tiles just to make me insane. Although I have only been here for some hours, it feels as if days or weeks have passed. I have barricaded myself to the point where I cannot even tell whether it is day or night. However, time seems very trivial now and the only thing that really matters is to stay alive and pray that someone will eventually find me. Should this not happen very soon, I fear that my days will be at an end.

My profession is of a somewhat doubtful character for I work as a treasure seeker although most people would not hesitate to call me a tomb raider. Yes, it is true that I excavate ancient tombs in the hope to find riches but it is in people's last resting places that you may find the greatest treasures. Over the years, I have found several artifacts that have proved to be of great value, and by selling those I have collected a tidy sum. These artifacts, however, cannot be sold on the common market since my line of work is considered unholy and sacrilegious and is therefore illegal.

My horrible fate began with a rumor. An old hermit living on the northwest hillside of the small town of Tann had died under mysterious circumstances and some townsfolk spoke of murder while others told tales of dark rituals of satanic worshiping. I, of course, did not believe any of it. It is simply one of those cases where an old man is being demonized just because of his choice of living in loneliness instead of adjusting to the social standards and associating with the other townspeople. The only rumor that truly interested me was the fact that he was told to be rich beyond imagination and that he, in his last will, insisted on having some of his most precious possessions brought with him in the family mausoleum. Excavating such a recent tomb sure was controversial so I realized that I would have to do it in total secrecy.

It was an early November morning when I arrived at the dull and silent town of Tann. The air was damp and there was a thick fog surrounding every building in the town like a python constricting its prey and very few people were to be seen. I made my way to a local hostel and booked a room for one night. It was quite obvious that the town did not have many tourists especially at this time of the season for the manager looked at me with most skeptic eyes and he quickly scanned me from my feet to my head and his eyes fell upon my backpack which I realize was oddly large for a one-night accommodation.

"I'm just passing through," I said casually, and I could see that his body relaxed. It was a comment he was used to and it was something he could easily comprehend. He gave me the key and I passed the counter to the staircase leading to the rooms.

"Most people do," I suddenly heard behind me.
"What?"

"Most people who come here only pass through. No one wants to stay," the man replied.

"Is that so?" I said, trying to sound polite.

"There is something wicked going on in this place. Most people will not speak of it but it is true," the hostel manager continued.

"Aha," I said, hoping it would end the conversation. The solicitude of the place had obviously made him delirious.

"It's that damn, old fool's fault," he continued. "He got himself mixed up in things no man should meddle with and now the whole bloody town's cursed because of him."

"Oh really?" I replied, trying not to sound as if I was judging him too hard, which I probably was. "Well, I need to be going now," I added and hurried up the stairs. I could see that he was about to continue but I had no desire to stay and chat with a complete stranger.

The room was simple and well enough for my purpose of being here. There was a wore-down bed and a wobbly nightstand next to it. In the corner of the room was a leather chair with suspicious stains on it. I avoided putting my things on it and then I decided to leave the room to take a closer look at the town mostly to avoid the manager, so I just left my backpack and then I swiftly made my way out.

There was a ghastly silence across the town, and it gave me goosebumps. In my line of work, I have visited many graveyards and burial grounds but even they were filled with more life than this place. I began regretting ever coming here and whatever treasure was buried in that godforsaken mausoleum did not feel worth the effort. However, it was too late to go back now and I decided I might as well do what I came for and then leave town in the cover of darkness since I did not feel like overstaying my welcome.

Suddenly, a local passed me by. It was so unexpected that he had me startled before I could speak my mind. For a moment far too long, I stood and inspected the young man before I said anything. I briefly asked him where the old man, whose tomb I was about to examine, had lived. The face of the young man turned pale as if I had asked him to commit a crime most foul and then he pointed to a hill further down the road.

"But, sir, you do not want to go there," the young man said.

"Because of the old man?" I asked, trying to sound casual.

"He is no ordinary man," the man emphasized. "He and his whole family are insane! Do you know that they even have their family grave in the backyard? Creepy!" Suddenly, I became a lot more interested.

"Really, you don't say?"

"Yeah, rumor has it that the freaks even built a tunnel from the house to the graves. Can you imagine that?" I shook my head, thanked him for the warning, and decided to take a stroll down the road to see what I could find.

All of a sudden, the road ended, and the only thing left was a small path leading away from the town. I followed the path and after a kilometer or so, the surroundings cleared up and I could see the house, although I should say manor given its size.

In my line of work, one is not startled easily, but even I have to admit that the sight before me right now had me shivering down to my very core for before me, was a manor so evil-looking it might have come directly out of some horror flick. The abomination of a building that was in front of me had me hesitating about moving forward but I decided that I needed to take a closer look and so I carefully approached the manor.

I soon realized why the place was so vicious-looking for there was simply nothing living about it. All of the flowerbeds had withered and only small fragments of decay were still there as proof of once-blooming flowers, and the grass which surrounded the house seemed bleak as if it had been drained of all its life. The color of the house, or rather the absence of color gave the facade a rotten kind of look and all of this put together made the building almost unbearable to set eyes on and my blood ran cold by the very knowledge that I even considered entering the tomb to the owner of this house.

Slowly and with a great deal of respect, I decided to take a closer look at the insides of the horrid beast. The stair leading up to the door was solid rock and almost completely covered in moss and various plants. The door itself was a massive thing made out of, what looked like huge logs of oak and it did not budge easily. After having been forced to use some of my more controversial methods to get inside, the door finally creaked open. There must have been an open window somewhere in the house for a cold wind passed me as I entered the hallway.

It was dark and silent apart from a light wind that persisted and seemed to come from the second floor and the electric light seemed to be malfunctioning.

For the best, I thought, reluctant to have nosy neighbors checking the house. I took out a small flashlight I always kept in my pocket just in case and shone around me. Dark wallpapers with twisted medallions which, in this dim light, looked just like people screaming in agony, covered the walls all the way down to the next room and I swear that I could hear their tormented voices like faint echoes through the room. I felt an ice-cold shiver running down my spine and I quickly pressed on, hoping to find something more ordinary in the next room.

My mind was already beginning to slip, and I must admit I felt somewhat paranoid but, nonetheless, I continued my exploration of this cursed lair. Suddenly, a voice filled the air. It was weak but I could clearly make out the words "Save me" like a soft breeze whispering in my ear. It was coming from the second floor, and I remember thinking that this was one of those times where you should listen to your instincts and run for it but for some reason, I did not. Instead, I felt a strange need to examine the voice, and being drawn to it I began making my way up the winding staircase. While walking up the stairs, I could hear the familiar sound of raindrops falling against the roof tiles and the sound increased as I approached a room just above the staircase. The door to the room was ajar and I carefully pushed it wide open. It was a plain bedroom and the window had been left open which made the room freezing cold. I went up to the window and tried to close it. I was sure that the caretaker must have left it open when they cleared out the belongings of the old man for the window was stuck and it took quite an effort to get it loose. Finally, it suddenly slammed shut and at the same time, there was a giant flash of lightning filling the room with bright, dazzling light.

I must admit it had me startled for I ran as quickly as I could to the ground floor and entered the room adjacent to the hallway. It was a library decorated in old Victorian style with bookshelves along every wall and on the other side of the room was a suitable fireplace. The whole room gave the impression of a man who had some style. I let my flashlight scan the room and that was when I saw it. The chair in the middle of the room, just beneath the chandelier and the noose from which they must have found him hanging. It was a bizarre sight and then, all of a sudden, another flash of lightning, far greater than the last one and in the middle of the thunder, a terrible shriek echoed in the night and I could see before me as clearly as brightest daylight, the old man trapped in the noose, screaming in terrible agony as he was being eaten by maggots from inside out. Then, as the lightning stopped, the old man vanished again as if he had never been there.

This was far more than my mind could bear so I ran for the door and decided to abandon all ideas of treasure for treasure is worth nothing if you are dead. When I came to the door it was shut tight and, no matter how I pushed, it simply would not open. I felt a rising panic inside of me and my breathing became more and more rapid. Suddenly, I felt as if someone gave me a hard push and I fell through a door and down a staircase leading to what I can only assume was the basement. It was pitch black apart from my flashlight which I had dropped in the fall.

After some difficulties, I managed to get back on my feet. I picked up the flashlight and examined the surroundings. The basement was extremely narrow, and the ground was nothing but hard-packed soil. Finally, my eyes fell upon a tunnel leading away from the house. It was dark and my flashlight could only illuminate the entrance. However, I decided that I had had enough of adventures so I went back up the stairs to leave nut when I came up, the door to the basement was shut tight and appeared to be barred from the other side. My blood froze from the sheer thought of who might have done it. It did not matter much though because now I was stuck with only one choice left. I had to go through the tunnel in hope of finding a way out. It was with a heavy mind I ventured into the darkness with nothing but a faint light to guide me.

Suddenly, the tunnel ended and I came to a room that could only be described as something out of the worst nightmare possibly imaginable. The ground was packed with the same kind of dark soil and the entire room was filled with tombstones. I took a few steps in order to get a better look. All of the stones had the surname "Smith" carved into them and as I raised my flashlight, I saw that it was not a room as much as it was a hall. An endless mausoleum of the entire family. Slowly I ventured forward deep into the dark until I came to a tomb significantly larger than the others and on it was the words "Here lies

Walter Smith" carved. I walked up to it but stumbled on what I assumed was a root of some sort. It was not until I grabbed my flashlight and shone upon it that I realized that it was a bone sticking out of the ground.

I reached for it and tried to pull it out. It seemed stuck and I grabbed it with both hands to force it out. Suddenly, it came loose and the entire ground started shaking as if it was a boiling pot and from within the graves, a thousand birds emerged. These birds, however, were not like any birds I have ever seen before for they were black like crows or ravens but their feathers were leathery like the skin of a bat, and instead of eyes they had black holes which seemed to perceive all around them. All of a sudden, they all turned to me and started screaming and I swear that their ghastly voices sounded almost human. Abruptly they fixed their hollow eyes upon me and charged. I ran for the life of me with the creatures right behind me. They flew in mad anger and their shrieks were like piercing arrows and I fled as fast as I could back up to the door when I suddenly remembered that it was barred. With nowhere else to go I continued up the staircase only to find that the door now was wide open. I ran out of the infernal mansion and out on the lawn. When I turned around to see the horrifying creatures burst out of the mansion in throngs turning the sky pitch black, I cried out and my body felt cold as if all blood had left. With my last remaining strength, I hurried and took shelter inside the woodshed where I have been ever since. I pray that someone will find me before it is too late…

In bloom

Karen took a badly needed puff on her fifth cigarette in what seemed like an eternity, but really was an all too short a time to justify the consumption. Although she already exceeded her normal daily intake, Karen felt that it was fully justified when she once again had been sent out on an assignment out in the middle of nowhere just because some over-enthusiastic woman in menopause got the idea to call Karen's editor just to propose that they would do an article about some small flower festival that no one would spend a single moment to read about.

Angrily, she pounded her hand on the steering wheel while smoking with an intense fury causing her to almost burning both the filter and her fingers. Life was unfair she had decided and she knew that this was the editor's way to get back at Karen for maybe expressing her contempt for small towns in the countryside and their population a little too clearly. Karen, however, was not ashamed of her opinion. She was honest. Something that many people confused with cruelty. She knew very well that she was often perceived as cruel and she might have been a bit harsh but the fact was that she never had enjoyed staying outside of town even for a simple weekend. Ironically, some said since she worked for a magazine called "Rustic homes on the countryside" which focused on articles often about how to get your flower beds to look outstanding in three simple steps or how to turn your patio into a cozy paradise.

Finding a job was not easy and although Karen was happy to have a job, she did not have the blind passion for home fixing as the rest of her colleagues. On the other hand, none of the others at her job was as highly educated as her and they definitely did not have the same ambitions to get ahead in their careers and most of all away from that horrible energy-sucking newspaper. At times Karen almost felt like Hercules, fighting her way through the labors given to her by the paper just to put her to the test.

The road in front of her felt like a maelstrom that drew her deeper and deeper into the seemingly endless forest without the opportunity to ever escape. She glanced down at her mobile as the last link to civilization but across the screen, she could read "911 call only". Karen swore. She could have figured out that the nearest cell tower was several miles away.

Now and then a house appeared along the road and she suffered silently with the poor devils who had chosen to live out here. She wondered what kind of people might live like this and envisioned perverted old men with sexual desires that bordered on pedophilia and alcoholics with hygiene so poor that it caused their teeth to rot down inside leaving a zombie-like appearance with needs as basic and grotesque as a zombie. As her next thought, she imagined a combination of everything and shivered at her own wild imagination. One thing was clear though. She no longer felt pity for the misfits living out here.

Suddenly Karen was stunned by a sight so distinctive and unusual that she almost drove off the road and into the ditch. On the right side of the road, a big house tinted up in a clearing in the forest. The house itself had a brownish tone and was nothing particularly fancy but the garden of the house had her completely amazed. So many times, she had been on awards which crowned the most beautiful garden or the year's most well-made flower bed, but even the most award-winning gardens resembled poor school projects compared to this. Without even spending as much as a single thought on the embarrassing festival she drove onto the driveway to get a closer look.

Garth lifted the beam from the door to the shed and went in to get more fertilizer for the flower beds. Ever since his wife died, he had taken great pride in keeping the flowers she loved so much, alive. Although she could no longer see the flowers, he was sure she would have appreciated his passionate commitment to keeping her life's work blooming. She had begun to grow roses of pure chance and now they grew all over the yard in all possible colors.

The thought of his wife made the job a little more bearable, and he bent down over the barrel where he kept the fertilizer. The past year had been ruthless and had claimed the lives of many plants, and he gazed down on the pitiful amount of fertilizer that was left. The rest had been spent just to keep all roses alive. It was apparent that he would need to replenish the supply in the near future and he heaved a deep sigh as the work to refill demanded much planning and effort.

Suddenly he was interrupted in his thoughts by the familiar, however, the infrequent sound of a car driving up to his house. A bit taken by surprise, he went out to see who could possibly come all the way out here. The car seemed to be new which alone proved that the driver was not from around here. Garth tried to get a grip on himself and went down to greet his guest.

The woman driving the car was energetic, to say the least, and explained that her name was Karen and wondered if she could make an article about his garden. Garth did not even have time to think, much less answer any of her clearly improvised questions. All of a sudden, she pulled out a camera and a notepad and went around and photographed every bush she saw. Garth was preoccupied with other thoughts and did not feel that he had time to chat with the woman.

Karen did not bother to try and make small talk. After all, she did not stop for a coffee or to chat about the weather. She only stopped to make a quick article and then be off again. Garth seemed to be an okay fellow, she thought, but slow like the rest of the population out here. He clearly was not aware of the quality of his garden and Karen did not want to give him too much credit. Seemed unnecessary. If she had seemed enthusiastic about the place, then it was only because of the garden and not the rat-infested excuse of a house. Suddenly, she heard Garth just behind her saying, "Where was this magazine you said?"

"New York," the woman replied without taking any more notice of the man.

"And you have a family there?"

"No, God, no. Just me."

"Is that so?"

Normally, Karen was not fond of sharing private information with strangers, and in most other situations she might have reacted to the odd question but she was still charmed about the garden and had many more questions that she wished to have answered so she let it pass. She put on her most selling smile and she even did her best to sound interested.

"So how do you get your roses this incredibly beautiful and big?"

"Well, it is important to have the right kind of fertilizer," Garth said with a slight smile on his face while his eyes wandered over her body. Karen did not know exactly why but there was something in the way that he looked at her that made her uneasy and she shuddered. In an attempt to shift focus, she began photographing a blood-red rose bush with fabulous thorns. Apparently, it worked for Garth excused himself and went off to the tool shed.

Karen was used to men undressing her with their eyes at the pub but there she was in an environment with plenty of other people who could step in if someone got too close. Here it was different. No one knew that she was here, and no neighbor was to be seen for several kilometers. It was obvious to Karen that the man liked what he saw, and even if he did not do anything more than look, it still had her shaken up badly. She tried not to care and focused on taking more pictures.

Without any time to react or feel pain, everything suddenly went black and she dropped the camera and fell to the ground. She woke up with a horrible headache and her white top was stained with fresh blood. Karen did her best to try and understand what was going on but everything was still blurry. She focused all her energy and saw that he had tied her hands up and hung her from a tree.

"Please don't take it personally," she heard from below. "It's just that people are so good for plant growth." Without really understanding what he meant, she looked down below her. There was an impact shredder with sharp blades. "If it is any consolation, this will be your chance to give something back to nature. Please believe me when I say that it is not of any insane pleasure that I do this. I simply need more fertilizer." While he said the last words, he slowly began to haul her down while the impact shredder chewed mercilessly below her.

The Manifest

It has been several weeks since my horrible deed, and I can still recall the foul smell of gunpowder and flesh. The left shoulder still hurts from the recoil and I am forced to eat heavy sedatives just in order to get at least a few hours of sleep. My dreams of late are far beyond any nightmare anyone could possibly imagine even in their wildest and most perverted dreams.

I will say it clearly right away so that there is no confusion for whoever reads my notes. I have committed a murder in cold blood and, still, I believe my actions to be justified and right. I want to add from the beginning that I do not consider myself as being mentally ill or even criminal. My hope is that by writing this you will come to see things my way and understand why I had to make the decisions I made.

It must be over a year ago that I had the great pleasure of meeting a young man by the name of Stephen Wall. His name did not mean much to me at the time as he was only another student starting his first term at the university where I used to teach. His major was history and to be more precise, the history of wars which happens to be my specialty.

It did not take him long to make himself at home and I remember him as a frequent visitor to the university library and already then, I thought that he could have a bright future in the field if he kept his studies up. As soon as I started teaching him, I remember how easy everything seemed to come to him. He had the most amazing ability to pick up details that others would miss. Insignificant things that someone perhaps mentioned vaguely in a context seemed to stick in his mind like glue.

He performed with perfect accuracy on every exam and engaged in lively debates about everything from political issues to poetry. It did not take him long to become somewhat of a role model for the other students and I must say that he also brought out the best in me. I found myself wanting to give my very best lectures every time he walked into the classroom, and I remember that I thought already then that he was far brighter than most other students.

The horrible events which finally led to both mine and his decay occurred just a short while after we had finished reading the section about World War I. I had just given the students their results back and Stephen was flawless as usual. He had, however, started to develop a certain cockiness you all too often find with gifted students and I could clearly see a glimpse of contempt toward those students who did not pass or barely made it. Looking back, I regret not speaking to him about it at the time but I also realize that there was no possible way for me to know what was about to come.

The following subject in my class was World War II. A subject that is just as grim as it is interesting. I had made a collection of the most important texts and started the course with routine-based certainty of someone who has taught the subject a thousand times. However, I must admit that I felt a bit eager to see how well Stephen would perform, but all the time a nervous feeling dwelled inside of me. The Holocaust is a sensitive subject to many students and I did not think of Stephen as the warmest and loving person.

Stephen immediately took a great interest in the class and even read the optional texts suggested in the course syllabus. He spent every waking hour in the library borrowing all of the books that he could possibly find on the Holocaust. At first, I did not think much of it. I was glad he had found a subject that could be the foundation to further research studies and as long as he spent his time studying, I only considered it to be a healthy way to practice the mind.

It was not until some weeks later that I started getting complaints from the other students regarding odd behavior and inappropriate comments from Stephen. It was not only the students who had noticed it, for I too saw a huge difference in his personality but it was not in his manners for he was still very polite and greeted me with respect every time he saw me. No, it was more in the discussions during the seminars that I could tell that he was changing. It was mainly some things that he would point out or say. Not right out but in a very subtle way which made it hard to tell what he really thought about the subject. I spoke to him about it and he assured me, in the calmest way that I had nothing to worry about. Thinking of it now makes me feel so naive.

After that brief conversation, it was quiet around him for a while and I was filled with a sense of feeling that his respect for me as a teacher and our little chat had made him more laid back. Then the accusations began once again and this time far more intense and serious. Students began expressing a feeling of being watched as if someone was following them around and some of them even expressed a fear of going out after dark. Up until now, it had only been feelings of unease among the students but not one of them had actually been a victim of any crime but as soon as the thought was out in the open, it was like turning on a switch, and all of a sudden, several reports started to come in.

At first, it was just pieces of paper containing threats but after a while, some of the students found dead animals in their rooms. Their throats had been cut and the body stabbed several times. Since it was so clear that it was a threat, the police were brought in but no evidence could be found. One of the threats that really got stuck in my mind was a young girl named Jess. She was a frequent member of the debate team and fought for animal rights. It was a late night and she came back from her studies. When she came home to her room, she could see that the door had been broken down. For some reason, she decided to walk in. The shriek could be heard over a thousand miles and sent shivers down my spine although I was in the other part of the university. I ran there as fast as I could only to find that someone had smeared gallons of blood all over her room. Even the ceiling was covered in dark, red blood. It took intense psychiatric care to get her back on her feet again.

The police investigated as usual but nothing could ever be linked to Stephen who always seemed to have a good answer for every question anyone would give him. I cannot say I was surprised. His witted tongue and skills in rhetoric had made him extremely hard to fool and I knew that he was way too smart to allow someone to trick him.

Stuck with no clues and very few options left the school decided to upgrade their security with more guards wandering the campus area. A totally understandable gesture but also completely useless. Right now, the students were innocent girls roaming London and he was Jack the Ripper, always one step ahead of the police. Although I did not have any evidence linking him to the events, I felt in my guts that he was the guilty one and it was only a matter of time before something really bad would happen.

The days went by and I started to calm down again. Stephen was still in my class but held a low profile and only spoke when spoken to. He was a complete outcast now and the other students had started making up names about him such as "the gravedigger," and "the reaper". The topic for the day was labor camps and I showed them some archive footage of how the German soldiers treated the Jews and in one particular scene, a German Nazi beats a little boy to death. The scene is very brutal so I can understand that many of my students have a problem watching it. But one girl took a real offense to the movie and screamed out in sheer disgust. It was then I heard. He did not say anything, it was not even a whisper. More like a sigh or a breath but you could clearly make out two words: "Drama queen." The girl was furious, and I had to stop her from tearing Stephen to pieces.

After that, there was a series of meetings with the principal, and Stephen had to explain his behavior and as always, he gave a most touching speech about feeling worn out and depressed. The principal bought it, of course. I had been there too. I knew the feeling when he spoke to you and how easy it was to take his side since he was always so very reasonable. The girl, however, did not buy his story. She did not say anything, but I could see it in her eyes. She knew that he meant exactly what he had said. I knew that too and this time I was really concerned for him.

It was in the middle of November and the weather outside was dark and gloomy which is also the main reason why I do not like that particular month. It was evening and I was reading when, suddenly, the phone rang. I took my time to answer it and when I finally did, I could hear the voice of one of the campus guards. He was stressed and struggling to catch his breath and the only words he could say was "you have to come here now." I do not think that I have ever driven that fast ever before. It was a miracle I did not hit anything.

When I finally parked my car, a thought came to me. It was a big university and the guard did not specify where I should go. However, that was something I did not have to think about for very long for I could already see the lights from several police sirens just by the forest next to the campus. I ran there as fast as possible and as I came closer, I could see the headmaster talking to a detective. I had enough time to think that whatever this was, it was bad.

What I saw in that forest could have the blood of any person freeze to ice, and as I saw what I am about to describe to you, I was filled with a deep feeling of helplessness, and my legs crumbled beneath me. It was the girl from my class whom Stephen had called a drama queen. She hung from a tree and her body was stabbed so badly that it almost fell apart. Just the mere sight of her was bad enough for my psyche, but then a most horrid smell found its way up my nostrils. It was the scent of dead meat and feces. I ran to the nearest bush in pure instinct when I suddenly heard the headmaster introduce the detective to me. Quickly, I managed to get a grip and greeted the young policeman. The headmaster had already told them about the incident in my class and how Stephen had apologized to the girl for his behavior.

Stephen was pointed out as "a person of interest" and was interrogated several times and in every conversation he had with the police, he assured them of his innocence and how deeply sorry he was for the poor girl. Still to this day, I do not know if he actually managed to convince the police or if they just lacked evidence, but I could tell that it would not be long until they released him, and then anything could happen. Stephen had gained a bad reputation all over the school, and some of the students even hated him. It was only a matter of time before something else like this would happen again. Then and there, I decided to take matters into my own hands.

Stephen was still in custody for the night so getting into his room was simple. I knew he would never leave evidence lying around to be easily found so I started looking in every drawer he had. The room was not big so finding evidence if there even was any, should be simple. But after having gone through every piece of paper, I still could not find a single thing that proved it to be him. I was starting to doubt myself but decided to make one final check before leaving the room, but when I turned around, I happened to stumble on a chair and fell to the floor and that was when I saw it. It was really hard to spot if you did not know where to look but one of the legs of the bed was hollow, and a brown envelope could be seen inside.

I pulled out the envelope and started reading. For each sentence, I felt more and more terrified for inside the envelope was an elaborate plan on a big attack against the university and how the university could be "purified from foreign blood" as he described it. I had a hard time understanding that what I was reading was the words of a student. Suddenly, I came to the part that hurt most of all. The part where he thanked me for all the ideas. I felt sick to my very soul and then I was filled with anger that I had never felt before and I decided to do something about him myself.

The next day Stephen was a free man since the police had no evidence against him. When I met him in the corridor at the university, he looked at me with a smile of triumph unaware of the fact that I had seen his notes. I pretended as if everything was completely normal and greeted him and he responded that he was very excited about continuing his studies. I still smiled and wished him all the best of luck. The bastard seemed to be well-rested and hardly affected by his terrible deed. I, on the other hand, had not slept at all, for I was up all night thinking about how to get him into my trap.

I needed something that was sure to interest Stephen enough to come undoubtedly so I had falsified a document which was made to look like a personal note of Adolf Hitler himself and told Stephen about my exclusive finding. His eyes sparkled like those of an excited kid who has found a treasure and although I felt sick inside, I stayed calm and invited him to come and see the document after school. When I told him that, he became so happy that I probably could have gotten him to confess to anything just to get a glimpse of the note.

Exactly at five, there was a knock at my office door and Stephen came in. There was something special about him now and it was clear that he was focused on the note because he acted as if I was not even in the room. Quickly he made his way to my desk and started reading the note with manic interest. His hands were shaking as he held the paper and he muttered silent words like "brilliant," and "fantastic," but as he came to the last line, he became mute and then started to chuckle as he turned toward me for the last line was a personal message from me to him just saying, "I know what you did." While he read the note, I had taken out the old six-shooter I usually only used at the firing range.

Stephen's eyes were furious and he had the look of a wild animal getting ready to attack his prey as he hissed to me, "You fool! You understand nothing! This is for the greater good!"

"Did you kill the girl for a greater good?" I asked him.

"Yes, of course! As I will with all of those who resist my cause! Do not tell me that you feel sorry for the girl!" I remained silent for a while as I gazed into the eyes of a madman I had once called brilliant and then pulled the trigger. It was a mess and pieces of flesh stained the window and my chair. I stood quietly for long and listened if I could hear any voices coming but it remained silent. It was late and my office is at the far end of the university. It took some time to clean up the mess and cover my tracks but I did it. Still to this day that scene with me and Stephen haunt me like a demon and I know that I will have to live with it for the rest of my life.

The Birth of a Psychopath

Before you go on reading any more of this letter, I feel obliged to tell you that never have I earlier in my life broken the law and my intentions have always been to live a peaceful life with my wife and although this letter will prove otherwise, I will have you know that I have always considered myself a sane person. With that said, we can continue.

You may recall a most dreadful and horrifying case a few months back. The papers wrote quite a lot about it. Several women fell victim to a murderer and cannibal known as the dead-end cannibal. As you may or may not remember, he was called that because he lured his victims into dead-end streets and feasted upon them. Only women were targeted and limbs, as well as intestines, were missing. I guess he had a taste for that.

I remember these events very well for you see, my wife, Jane Goodall, was one of the victims. She had been working late and decided to take a shortcut through some alleys and that was where she met him. It is quite funny really because I cannot recall where I heard about it first for the papers were there almost at the same time as the police and I can still remember that weird feeling when I saw my wife on the evening news. It was a bizarre and a most morbid sense of failing to comprehend the situation.

When the police summoned me to identify her body, I was filled with a whole set of new feelings I never knew a person could have. I stood at the morgue beholding the woman I had loved for so many years and still loved. She had an odd appearance as if her body was still processing what had happened to it. Although her heart had been carved out, she still looked surprised. Surprised and in shock over her defiled and mutilated destiny.

In her eyes, there was nothing of her warmth as a person, and the loving smile she could give a person that would make them like her in an instant was all gone. Now the only thing showing in her eyes was a never-ending fear that she was forced to take with her to the afterlife. I felt sadness and grief but more than anything else I felt anger and hatred toward the monster who had deprived us of a life of happiness. The hatred arose like a tide. An ever-growing storm within me that needed to be let loose.

There and then I made a commitment to avenge my bride and bring justice upon the life we could have had that was taken from us. I left the morgue with nothing else in mind than a growing desire for vengeance spreading like an infected wound in my body, and I realized what had to be done.

Tiffany was a prostitute, apparently, as she accepted money to follow me. She had none of my beloved wife's features, but she used the same perfume and, for that, I hated her making the deed I was about to do so much simpler. I imagine she was under the influence of some kind of substance because she never even questioned where we were going.

I took her to the nearest dead-end street and left her like Andromeda chained by the sea awaiting the monster to devour her. It took some time, and I began to think my effort had been all in vain. Tiffany was about to leave as she was tired of waiting for me to return but then from the shadows, I saw him. The predator, silently watching his prey, and just as he was about to lash out at her with all his rage, I made my move and shot him in the leg with my old hunting rifle.

Tiffany screamed and ran away for safety as my game stumbled and fell due to the shattered bone on his leg. But although it must have hurt tremendously, he did not scream. He did not even seem to be bothered by the fact that the wound was gushing out blood all over him. Yet to this day I do not know if it was hatred or fear of him that caused me to take the rifle and strike it against his head but he fell to the ground making it possible for me to collect my price.

The gunshot was sure to attract a crowd so I put him in the trunk of my car and drove off as fast as I could without causing suspicion. Having come this far, I wanted to make sure to keep any kind of law enforcement out of my business. At the moment, the only goal was to make my way home making it possible for me to proceed to stage two of my plan.

Finally home, I carried the wounded man into my house and down to the basement where I usually prepared and cut up whatever meat I had hunted. Most carefully I began undressing him whereupon I cuffed his hands together and hung him in one of the meat hooks. As I strung him up, he slowly awoke and although there was an honest sense of surprise in his eyes, he did not speak. To tell the truth, I found his lack of words frightening but I did my best to ignore my fear and instead, I told him the whole story and the reason as to why he was here. As I told him who I was, there was a glimmer of something else in the way he gazed upon me. A smug grin of pure satisfaction telling me that he was proud of his accomplishment. I then and there decided to wipe the grin off his face in the most horrid way possible.

Over the following days, I kept the beast strung up in my cellar. With no food and only water to keep him alive, he slowly began to show his true self as I could hear moans of starvation filling the halls of my house like a bittersweet symphony. For hours I would sit and listen to his unjustified lament but though it filled me with some sense of contentment I still could not put my heart at rest.

Spite the fact that I had explained the reasons for my deed he did not fully understand and felt my pain as the cries of hunger coming from the basement were cries of basic needs. He was hungry but not for any kind of food that I was willing to provide for him. If his creature would ever understand my sorrow, I needed to put his body and soul through a whole new world of torment. It was only just I figured. Whatever pain I could make him endure was miles away from my own and he had to understand the consequences of his behavior. Even if he failed to see my perspective causing him harm would still give me a sense of serenity.

Since I wanted him to fully feel my pain, I chose not to bring the meat cleaver from the kitchen but, instead, I took a small knife usually used to cut up fruits and vegetables whereupon I walked down into the basement.

I was happy to see a sparkle of hope in his eyes as he saw me. That meant I now had something I could rob him of and I felt a wave of exaltation arising like the tide as I imagined all the things I would do to make him understand.

Before me now stood the creature so vile and grotesque in all its abomination free to be inflicted by all my sorrow. There were very few human features left in his appearance making my task so much easier. Very slowly I began carving patterns into his skin with the fruit knife like a small child doodling with a crayon and for every time I let the blade cut into his skin, I could see just a little bit more of the hope in his eyes fading away.

He was bleeding quite heavily now as the blood dripped down on my white tile floor. I would have to clean here later. Suddenly he appeared to try and communicate with me very silently; he uttered a single word: food. When I calmly explained to him that there would be no food due to the fact that he ate my wife, he gazed at me in a way that told me he now realized that he would never leave the basement.

After a while longer, I grew tired of inflicting pain and went back upstairs. As I was about to go up the staircase, I heard him speak another word. Monster. I chose to ignore him and went up without replying. Back in the kitchen, I sat down to ponder the situation for a while. He was bleeding heavily and with no food or water, he would not be able to hold on for much longer. I could feed him but then again, why should he have the privilege to eat when both he and I knew the nature of his deeds that had put him in this situation in the first place? But then again, with no food, he would soon reach the end without fully understanding the graveness of his actions. Then it struck me. A way I could keep him alive.

I went back down to him and began carving off tiny stripes of flesh from his body that I threw to him and like a starved dog he literally devoured every piece and slice by slice he feasted upon himself in one last meal before the blood loss and the pain claimed his life.